D0444475

ANNA KERZ

BETTER THAN WEIRD

ORCA BOOK PUBLISHERS

Copyright © 2011 Anna Kerz

All rights reserved. No part of this publication may be reproduced or transmitted in any form or by any means, electronic or mechanical, including photocopying, recording or by any information storage and retrieval system now known or to be invented, without permission in writing from the publisher.

Library and Archives Canada Cataloguing in Publication
Kerz, Anna, 1947-
Better than weird / Anna Kerz.

Issued also in electronic format.
ISBN 978-1-55469-362-7

I. Title.
PS8621E79B48 2011 JC813'.6 C2010-907944-2

First published in the United States, 2011
Library of Congress Control Number: 2010941928

Summary: When Aaron's long-absent father returns, Aaron must cope with bullying at school, his grandmother's illness and his father's pregnant new wife. *Better Than Weird* is a stand-alone sequel to *The Mealworm Diaries*.

Orca Book Publishers is dedicated to preserving the environment and has printed this book on paper certified by the Forest Stewardship Council.

Orca Book Publishers gratefully acknowledges the support for its publishing programs provided by the following agencies: the Government of Canada through the Canada Book Fund and the Canada Council for the Arts, and the Province of British Columbia through the BC Arts Council and the Book Publishing Tax Credit.

Design by Teresa Bubela
Cover photography by First Light and Dreamstime
Typeset by Jasmine Devonshire

ORCA BOOK PUBLISHERS
PO Box 5626, Stn. B
Victoria, BC Canada
V8R 6S4

ORCA BOOK PUBLISHERS
PO Box 468
Custer, WA USA
98240-0468

www.orcabook.com
Printed and bound in Canada.

14 13 12 11 • 4 3 2 1

To Katie and Alex, who love stories and listen well

ONE

"Aaron!" Gran called from downstairs. "Are you up, Aaron?"

Aaron heard, but didn't answer.

"Aaron!" Gran called again, louder this time.

"Okay! Okay! I'm up." He flopped over and lay spread-eagled in his bed.

"Aaron Stewart Waite!" Gran hollered. "Get up right now!"

Sighing, Aaron patted his night table for his glasses and put them on before he rolled out of bed and stumbled out of the room. He was standing in front of the toilet when his grandmother called for the fourth time. "For goodness sake, Aaron! Close the door."

Aaron flushed, watching the water swirl before it swooshed away. He flushed a second time just to see the water spin. He would have flushed again, but a creak on the stairs warned him that Gran was on her way up. He closed the door.

"Hurry up, now," Gran said. "You don't want to be late again."

Aaron was pulling an arm out of his pajama sleeve when he noticed a tuft of hair sticking up on one side of his head. *It looks like a chimney*, he thought. *I have a chimney growing out of my head.* He chuckled and raked his fingers through the unruly tuft. The hair separated and flattened, then bounced back. He patted it gingerly with the palm of his hand. It would be funny if it stood up like that all day.

He was still chuckling when Gran said, "Aaron! Get in the shower—now!"

"Okay. Okay. Okay," he said, his head bobbing.

He stepped out of his pajama pants, climbed into the tub and closed the curtain. When the water ran warm, he pulled up the little toggle that made it pour from the showerhead. Then he stood, eyes closed, to let it pulse against his forehead. *Sounds like rain,* he thought. He began to sing tunelessly: "Rain, rain, go away. Come again another day."

He stopped, his head filled with thoughts of rain. "Not the day my dad comes home," he said out loud. "Don't come then."

"I'll be there before the end of November," his dad had said when he phoned. "And I'll bring a surprise."

"For me?" Aaron had asked.

"For you and for Gran."

"Is it big? Is it a big surprise?"

His father wouldn't tell.

Tipping his head back, Aaron opened his mouth and let the spray fill it. Then he spouted, sending a stream of water arching to the tiled wall. He laughed, then turned and let the spray thrum against the back of his head.

He could think of lots of things his father might bring for him…but for him *and* Gran? What could that be? What?

He turned again, face into the spray, until Gran called, "Aaron! Get moving!"

Gran was at the top of the stairs when he hurried past, a towel wrapped around his middle, his hair and body shedding water like rain. "I don't suppose you remembered to use soap this morning?" she said.

He grunted, jumped into his room and closed the door with his hip.

"Put on the clothes I laid out on your bed," she called as she started back down. "The stuff you wore yesterday is filthy. Put it in the laundry hamper."

He was almost dressed when he saw his underwear still neatly folded on the bed. "Oops! Forgot," he said. He wadded it up, intending to throw it into the hamper with yesterday's clothes. His arm went back for the toss, then stopped. Could he go to school without underwear? If Tufan knew, he'd say, *You're weird.*

Aaron heard the words so clearly, he glanced around in case Tufan had magically appeared in his bedroom. He was relieved to find himself alone. But in his head, Tufan's voice kept taunting. *Weird. Weird. Weird.*

"Am not," Aaron snapped. Hearing his own voice in the empty room made him feel silly. "I'm talking to myself," he said. Then he groaned, remembering something Tufan really *had* said: "His dad's gonna take one look and disappear all over again."

"Is not!" Aaron had shouted back. "He's coming back to stay! He said! He said!" But the words were a lie. His father had said he was coming, but he'd never once said he would stay.

I'll be good, Aaron thought. *I'll be so good he'll want to stay.*

He sighed. He knew how hard that would be. For one thing, he knew he talked too much. That's what everybody said. That's why they called him Aaron Cantwait.

"I'm not weird, just different," he muttered, repeating something Gran told him. "We can't all be the same," she often said. "You're just a little different."

Better than weird, he thought. Even so, he didn't want to be so different that his dad would come home after eight years away and then leave again.

With a little huff of frustration, he pulled off his pants and put on the underwear. Just in case.

He had his hand on the knob, ready to leave, when he saw the calendar tacked to his door. There were large red *X*s marked through all the days of November so far. He reached for the red marker on his bedside table and drew a new *X* through the box for November 16, then counted to the 28th. Twelve. His dad was coming home in twelve days. Twelve. Everything would be different once his dad was back. Everything.

Taped up beside the calendar were two lists. That's what his Big Brother, Paul, had told him to do. "If you want to organize your life, make a list," Paul had said. Aaron had listened.

Paul was different too. But he was cool different. Paul had two rings pierced into his right eyebrow.

He had a tongue stud, and he was talking about getting a tattoo. Paul knew stuff. He was in high school. If he said lists were good, Aaron was willing to make lists.

Things Dad will teach me

1. *how to hit a homerun*
2. *how to ride a bike*
3. *how to rollerblade*
4. *how to skateboard*
5. *how to kick a soccer ball*
6. *how to play the guitar*

Things to do with Dad

1. *go skiing*
2. *play baseball*
3. *visit the dinosaur exhibit at the museum*
4. *eat popcorn and watch all the Star Wars movies*
5. *visit the Science Center*

"Oh, Aaron," Gran said the first time she saw his lists. "You're expecting too much. Your dad…I'm not sure he'll be able to…" She stopped, then went on in a rush. "For sure he can't teach you to play the guitar. He doesn't know how to play himself."

"Okay," Aaron said. He drew a line through the last entry on the first list and added 6. *learn to play the guitar* to the second list.

Aaron counted the empty boxes on the calendar one more time, just to make sure. There were still twelve. He reached for the door.

"Oops!" he said. "Almost forgot." Turning back, he dropped to his belly and wriggled under his bed.

On the floor under the head of his bed was a cardboard box filled with dirt, home to his pet toad. "How you doin', Buddy?" Aaron asked as he looked into the box. "You okay?"

The toad, half-buried, stared back.

Aaron stroked the creature's head. The eyes closed. "You like that?" He stroked Buddy's head again.

Keeping a pet toad wasn't easy now that winter was coming, and keeping it a secret from Gran was even harder. He had been feeding it worms and bugs from the garden. Now bugs were getting hard to find. Luckily, he could still dig worms out of the compost bin. He just had to be careful to dig when Gran wasn't looking.

The doorbell rang.

"I'll bring you some worms after school," he said as he slipped the box back into place and backed out from under the bed. He scrambled to his feet and headed downstairs.

"It's Jeremy," he hollered as he went. "I gotta go. We're doing announcements."

"Announcements? You haven't even had breakfast," Gran called from the kitchen.

"Have to practice."

He had already struggled into his coat and was hoisting his backpack to his shoulders when Gran hurried into the hallway and blocked his way. He tried to get around her, but she refused to move. "Stand still and listen," she said. The sharpness in her voice made him look at her face. She was frowning, but she was also holding out two muffins. "Take these," she said. "You can eat on the way. And this is for recess." She held out an apple.

He stayed long enough for Gran to shove the apple into his backpack, but the whole time he was hopping from foot to foot. "Okay. Okay. Okay," he said, head bobbing.

He was out the door and scrambling down the porch steps before he thought to say goodbye. When he turned to wave, Gran was almost invisible, blurred by the fog that had formed on the glass of the storm door. He thought he saw her wave back, but he wasn't sure, and when Jeremy called, "You coming or what?" Aaron hurried to catch up.

TWO

Every year the grade-six class took on the job of making the morning announcements at school. On Friday afternoon, Mr. Collins had picked Jeremy to be responsible for the following week. "You can choose a friend to share the job," he had added.

That was all Aaron needed to hear. "Me! Me! Me! Pick me, Jeremy! Pick me!" he called out.

He saw Jeremy glance at Horace, who shrugged and shook his head. Jeremy sighed. "Okay. I'll do it with Aaron," he said.

All weekend Aaron felt lucky, and now that it was Monday, he felt even luckier. *Jeremy picked me,* he kept thinking. *He picked me to be his friend.*

In September, Jeremy had come from Nova Scotia and joined their class. Mostly he played with the boys, but sometimes he played with the girls too, and sometimes he walked Karima home.

"Do you like her?" Aaron asked one day.

"A little," Jeremy admitted. "She's really nice."

Aaron figured Jeremy liked Karima a whole lot. He thought Jeremy liked him a lot too. After all, they had done the mealworm study together and now they were working on the new science project about space. They were building a city with houses and launching pads and rocket ships.

Jeremy was good at stuff Aaron wished he could do: cross-country, volleyball, even skipping. When Mr. Collins started a skipping team, they both joined, and Aaron went to all the practices, even though skipping was hard for him.

Jeremy picked me, he thought as he hurried to catch up. *He picked me.*

"Here," he said, holding out one of Gran's muffins. "Banana. With raisins...and chocolate chips."

Jeremy took the muffin, and the boys ate as they walked on in silence.

When Aaron finished, he brushed the crumbs from his lips with the back of his hand. "He's coming in twelve days," he said. "My dad. You wanna meet him?"

Jeremy shrugged. "Maybe. I guess."

"When you come to my house, I'll show you my lists."

"Lists?"

"Yeah. It's all the stuff I'm gonna do with my dad. And if you want...you can think of stuff to do with my dad too. I'll just add it to the lists and we'll do it together. You and me and my dad."

"Maybe," Jeremy said, walking a little faster.

Aaron was confused. Why wasn't Jeremy excited? Didn't he want to do stuff with him and his dad? He licked his bottom lip as he tried to figure it out. When his tongue snagged against a loose flap of skin, he gnawed on it absently. The skin lifted, bit by bit, until it broke free. It hurt. He licked the sore spot, tasting the rusty tang of blood.

"Is Paul still gonna be your Big Brother when your dad comes back?" Jeremy asked.

"Paul?"

"Yeah. I just wondered, 'cause he was your Big Brother when you didn't have a dad, but when your dad comes back, what happens to Paul? Does he still get to be your Big Brother, or do the people at Big Brothers find him some other kid who doesn't have a dad?"

"I dunno." Aaron hadn't thought about losing Paul. Then he brightened. "Maybe when *my* dad comes back,

Paul can be *your* Big Brother. And he can be your Big Brother forever, 'cause your dad's dead, isn't he, so he's never coming back, right?"

Jeremy didn't answer. That confused Aaron, and they plodded the rest of the way to school in silence.

* * *

The school felt a little eerie so early in the morning. It was quiet without any other kids around, as if it was sleeping. Aaron was relieved to see Miss Chang, the kindergarten teacher, walk by. "Good morning, boys," she said. They said good morning back before she hurried away, her shoes *click*, *click*, *click*ing against the floor tiles.

They went straight to the office. The music teacher, Ms. Masilo, and the secretary were inside, talking. They looked happy. Jeremy waited. It was clear he didn't want to interrupt, so Aaron waited too. It felt like a long time before they were noticed and the secretary waved them in.

"What's the problem, boys?" she asked.

But before they could answer, Ms. Masilo snapped, "You should be outside. You're not allowed in the school before the bell."

Aaron was startled by Ms. Masilo's voice. *She was smiling a minute ago,* he thought. *What made her mad?*

“We’re doing the announcements this week,” Jeremy said. “Mr. Collins said he’d meet us in the office to show us how to use the PA system.”

“*You’re* doing the announcements?” Ms. Masilo looked right at Aaron.

“Mr. Collins said. He said we could,” Aaron managed to say.

“Yes, I did,” Mr. Collins said, coming up behind them. “Come on in, boys, and I’ll show you the ropes.”

“The ropes?” Now Aaron was really confused. “Do we have to skip while we make announcements?” he asked.

He heard Mr. Collins chuckle, and he saw Ms. Masilo’s painted-on eyebrows climb up her forehead. He guessed moving her eyebrows was something she did on purpose, and since Mr. Collins had laughed, he decided it would be good to join in. The sound that came from him started as a snort and turned into a high-pitched hoot. He stopped when he saw Ms. Masilo’s lips tighten. She made a face, not at him, but at Mr. Collins. Then she turned and left the office.

“Come here, Aaron,” Jeremy said, waving him over to where Mr. Collins was waiting by the PA system. “Pay attention. We don’t want to mess up.”

Mr. Collins showed them which buttons to push to make their voices heard in each of the classrooms.

Then he had them practice speaking into the microphone. "Testing. Testing. One, two, three," Jeremy said. When Aaron tried, his voice came through with a funny whistling sound.

"Don't get too close," Mr. Collins said. "You don't want to swallow the mike."

"Swallow the mike," Aaron echoed. The thought of swallowing something so large made him want to laugh, but Jeremy wasn't even smiling, so Aaron pressed his lips together and stayed silent.

They decided to divide the work. Jeremy would turn on the speakers and make the first two announcements, and Aaron would read the third and then turn everything off.

Mr. Collins made them read the announcements twice. "Remember now," he said before he left, "speak slowly and clearly so everybody knows what you're saying."

"Okay," Aaron said. He was determined to do this job right.

Once the final bell rang and all the kids were in the school, Jeremy turned on the speakers and played the anthem. Then he began the announcements. "From Mr. Collins, this message is for volleyball players: Please eat in the lunchroom, then meet at the gym doors at twelve fifteen. Remember your knee pads and running shoes.

"And from the principal's office: A reminder for teachers about the meeting for primary staff in the library at noon today." He stepped back to let Aaron move forward.

"Allissa, in grade one, has lost her library book," Aaron began. "If anyone finds a copy of *Buttercup's Lovely Day*, please take it to room 113 and Allissa will thank you." When he was done, Jeremy pointed to the power button and Aaron turned the PA off. He sighed. Everything had gone well.

They were on their way out of the office when two little girls arrived, holding hands and giggling. On their heads they wore the kind of paper crowns Miss Chang always gave kids on their birthdays. One of them carried a piece of paper. As Aaron stepped back to hold the door, the secretary said, "Aaron, wait. Miss Chang has sent this last-minute announcement."

So Aaron went back. He read the message, then pushed the button that turned on the speakers. "Here's a late-breaking announcement," he said. "There are two birthdays in the kindergarten. Kathryn and Fiona are both five years old today. Happy birthday, girls."

The girls giggled again, and Aaron felt good. He had done everything right. He hadn't repeated any of the words, not even the ones for the last announcement, which he hadn't practiced.

While he was smiling, an older woman came into the office. She was small and thin, and her gray hair hung down her back in a long braid. She was wearing what looked like a blue sari under her winter coat.

"I am bringing the lunch for my grandson," she said, passing a brown paper bag to the secretary. "That foolish boy. He forgets everything. He must stay to play volleyball at noon today, but he does not remember to bring his noonday meal."

"What's your grandson's name?" the secretary asked.

"Tufan. His name is Tufan."

"Do you know his teacher's name?"

The woman shook her head.

"Mr. Collins. Tufan is in Mr. Collins's class," Aaron piped up.

"Yes. Mr. Collins," the woman said. "I fear I am forgetful too. Like my grandson."

"I'll have Aaron take your grandson's lunch upstairs," the secretary said as she passed Aaron the bag.

The woman smiled. "You are in Tufan's class?" she asked. "Remind him to eat slowly. It is better for his digestion."

Aaron felt his face heat up at the thought of talking to Tufan about his digestion. He wanted to say, *No way*, but Tufan's grandmother said, "You are a very helpful boy. Thank you."

The words made Aaron feel proud, and what came out of his mouth was, "I'll...I'll tell him. I'll tell him to eat slowly."

The woman smiled, and then she left.

"Well done," the secretary said. Aaron beamed as he turned off the speakers.

When Aaron reached the upper hallway, Mr. Collins was talking to Karen, the school counselor. "Can you make time for him?" he was saying. "I'm not sure what's going on, but something's not right in that boy's life."

"I'll fit him in," she said. Then she looked up and smiled. "Good job, Aaron," she said.

"Yeah. Great job," Mr. Collins said, and Aaron bounced with joy the rest of the way to his classroom.

When he walked in, kids began to clap. Aaron almost took a bow, but a voice said, "Don't forget to remind Tufan to eat slowly."

"It's better for his digestion," someone else called out.

"That foolish boy forgets everything," mimicked a third. Then they laughed.

Aaron looked around. *They heard*, he thought. He was going to laugh too. It was pretty funny. Everybody hearing Tufan's grandmother talk about his digestion.

But all thoughts of laughter ended when Tufan stood up. "Shut up," he growled.

The class fell silent. Tufan's eyes narrowed until his brows made a dark V on his forehead. His nose twitched. Aaron had seen that once on the Nature channel when a tiger was stalking a deer. The tiger's nose twitched; then it pounced and the deer died.

Hand shaking, Aaron held out the paper-bag lunch and braced himself. Tufan came closer.

"Come on, Tufan," Jeremy called out. "Forget about it. It was no big deal."

Tufan paused, and Aaron held his breath.

That's when Mr. Collins walked into the room. "Sorry I'm late," he said. "Let's get started."

Tufan snatched the bag from Aaron's fingers. "This isn't over, Cantwait," he muttered. "You're dead meat."

"Yeah," Aaron said, thinking about the tiger's muzzle buried inside the deer's belly. "Dead meat."

THREE

"Let's trade jobs," Jeremy said on Tuesday morning. "You start the announcements today and I'll finish them."

"You think I'm gonna mess up again," said Aaron.

"I just want to make sure."

"That I don't mess up."

"That you...yeah...that you don't mess up and get into more trouble. Tufan's still mad. I know leaving the mike on was no big deal, but he didn't like it. Don't talk to him. He'll get mad no matter what you say. Just stay out of his way till he gets over it."

"Okay. I'll go first. And you remember to switch off the speakers so nobody turns you into dead meat."

"Okay," Jeremy said. But that morning, nothing went wrong, and Mr. Collins said that for the rest of the week they wouldn't have to come in as early. "Just come to the office a few minutes before the bell rings to read over the announcements," he told them.

* * *

Jeremy was right about Tufan. He was still mad. "Stay out of my face," he told Aaron in the hallway as the class got ready for recess.

Aaron wanted to say, *You're a bully and you don't scare me*. That's what Mr. Collins had told them to say when he talked to the class about bullies. He said bullies don't hurt people who stand up for themselves.

Aaron stared at Tufan's dark hair, gelled to stand in spikes, and at the fine hairs sprouting on Tufan's upper lip. Then Tufan's nose twitched, and Aaron shivered.

"C'mon, Aaron. Let's go," Jeremy said. He walked between them, breaking the spell, and Aaron was able to turn and follow Jeremy out.

In spite of Tufan's threat, Aaron felt good as he scrambled down the stairs. Jeremy was watching out for him. *My friend. My friend,* he thought. But as soon as they passed through the outer door, Horace called, "Hey, Jer, wanna be on my team? You can play first base."

Jeremy looked out to the field, then back at Aaron. "You wanna play soccer baseball with us?" he asked.

Aaron was going to say yes, but before he could say anything, Tufan brushed by and raced toward the diamond. In the field the boys were already organizing teams. As he watched, Aaron realized not one of them would want him on their team. They would complain. They'd yell every time he dropped the ball and when he didn't kick hard enough. He shook his head. "Not today," he said.

Jeremy shrugged and hurried to join Horace's team.

For a while Aaron stood alone. Around him, kids were skipping or tossing tennis balls against the wall. Little kids were laughing and playing tag. Everybody was playing with somebody. Except him. There was nobody for him.

He walked to the side of the yard. There he followed the wire-mesh fence until he reached a tree surrounded by a drift of leaves. They were damp with the morning dew. When he marched through the pile, kicking his feet to make them fly, they rose, then plopped back to earth in wet clumps. It was no fun.

He moved on. Beside the fence he found a thin branch that he whipped back and forth. It made a whistling sound. "I'll get you this time, Darth Vader," he said, lunging the way he had seen Luke Skywalker do in the movies. When he tired of that, he dragged the twig along the fence to make a different sound. He lurched along, across the back of the yard and down the far side, so busy listening to the sound of the branch he forgot everything else. A soccer ball rolled across his path and stopped beside him.

"Get the ball!" a voice called out.

Aaron looked around.

"Get the ball!"

Grinning, he picked it up.

"Throw it!" the voice yelled.

Other voices yelled too. "Throw it! Throw the ball!"

Aaron heard the words. He looked toward the baseball diamond.

"Throw, Aaron!" Jeremy shouted. So Aaron threw, but with the twig in his hand he didn't have a good grip. The ball dribbled through the grass and stopped, not two feet away. The boys laughed. Aaron laughed too, until he saw Tufan coming for it. He wanted that ball to be away from him when Tufan reached it, so he pulled back his leg to give it a kick. Some kind of magic must have happened then, because his toe connected and the ball hurled forward, hard and straight.

"Yes!" Aaron shouted, punching the air.

His short celebration ended when the ball crashed into Tufan's middle. A kind of *HUH!* sound came from his mouth when it hit, and he leaned forward, gagging.

"You okay?" boys called as they hurried to his side.

Tufan's arm brushed them away. "You're de—," he started, his words interrupted by a cough. "You… really are…dead meat," he said, as he staggered toward Aaron.

Aaron saw Jeremy come running. Saw Jeremy's hand grab Tufan's arm. "Come on," he heard Jeremy say. "It was an accident. You know he can't kick. He didn't do it on purpose."

"Your team's up, Tufan," Horace called. "You coming?"

Tufan paused. He pointed at Aaron. "Stay away—" He coughed again. "Stay away from me unless you have some kind of death wish."

"Go, Aaron," Jeremy called out. "Just go."

So Aaron jogged away. He didn't stop until he got to the school doors. When he looked back, the guys were playing as if nothing had happened.

FOUR

Every Tuesday before lunch, Aaron went to see Karen, his counselor. Karen had a teacher name. It was Mrs. Matthews, but right at the beginning she had said, "You can call me Karen when we're working together." So he did. He liked her name because it rhymed with his. Sometimes he said the two names over to himself. "Karen, Aaron." They sounded good together.

Lately Karen had been helping him to do something she called *reading faces*.

"It's like reading a book," she had told him, "but instead of reading the words on a page, you read the expressions people wear on their faces. Their expressions give you clues about what they're thinking or feeling. When you know how someone's feeling, it's easier for you to say and do the right thing."

"It would be better to read minds," Aaron said. "If I could read minds, I would know *everything* people are thinking." He closed his eyes, pressed his fingers against the sides of his head and pretended he could hear Karen's thoughts.

"Like, right now you might be thinking, 'I wish I had a double-fudge ice-cream sundae,' and if I could read your mind, I'd say, 'Let's blow this joint and get a double-fudge ice-cream sundae,' and you'd say, 'Wow! Aaron. You knew exactly what I was thinking!' And then we'd go to the ice-cream store to get one."

Karen laughed. "*Let's blow this joint*?"

"Yeah. Sometimes they say that in the movies. *Let's blow this joint*."

Karen laughed again. "Wow! Aaron. You knew exactly what I *was* thinking!"

Then Aaron laughed too, because he knew she was joking. But when Karen stopped laughing, he kept on until she put up her hand like a stop sign and said, "Enough already."

He stopped. "Wasn't it funny?"

"It was," Karen explained. "But it's not anymore. Jokes get old fast. That joke is so old now, it's dead.

Besides, we can't blow this joint until we're finished today's exercise, so let's get to it."

Aaron wasn't ready. "I read your mind!" he said. "I read it. I did." Then he hooted and said, "Ya wanna blow this joint?"

Karen moved to stand behind him. She put both her hands on Aaron's shoulders and turned him to look into the mirror hanging on the wall of her small room. "Aaron, look at my face," she said.

Aaron studied her face in the mirror. Her eyebrows were scrunched together and her mouth was a tight line, the ends pointing down. "You're making a mad face. Are you mad at me?"

"No, I'm not mad at you, but you're right. I'm making a mad face. Can you think of something to do if someone makes a mad face at you?"

Aaron's shoulders drooped. "Probably I should run, 'cause they might turn me into dead meat."

Karen's frown deepened. "Has someone been hurting you?" she asked.

"Not yet," Aaron said.

"Someone threatened to hurt you?"

"Only if I keep acting weird. But I'm gonna stop."

Karen took her hands from Aaron's shoulders. "Aaron," she said, "if someone has threatened you, we should know. Mr. Ulanni suspends students for that."

"Suspended from the neck until dead!" Aaron said. "Like in the pirate movies."

"No! Of course not. They're suspended from class."

"But then...then they come back, right?"

"Yes. They come back. But the school works with them, and with their parents, to improve their behavior."

"You mean, like you work with me?"

"A little like that, but probably not the same."

"When my dad comes, are you gonna work with him? 'Cause he's my parent, right?"

"When he comes, I'd like to meet him."

"Yeah," Aaron said. He stared into the mirror. There was a worried look on his face. What would she tell his dad anyway?

"Aaron? Are you there, Aaron?" Karen asked.

He turned to her.

"Every time you've talked about your dad coming home, you've been excited. Aren't you excited anymore?"

He scrunched his eyebrows together, tightened his lips and made the ends turn down. "See that?" he said. "Does it look like a mad face?"

"You've got it. That's a mad face all right. Did something I said make you mad?"

Aaron got up and walked around the room examining the posters on the walls before he came back. "Tufan made a mad face," he said.

"At you? Did he make a mad face at you?"

Aaron shrugged.

"When someone is mad at you, there are things you can do besides run away. Can you think of any?"

He shook his head, no.

"If they're mad because of something you did, you might say 'sorry.' It never hurts to apologize."

"Okay. I can do that. Maybe. I guess."

A bell rang.

"Lunchtime," Aaron said.

"Yes," Karen said. "Lunch." She sighed. "Remember now, if someone is hurting you, or threatening to hurt you, we're all here to help. You can tell me, or Mr. Collins or even Mr. Ulanni. Okay?"

Aaron nodded.

"What are you going to remember?"

He huffed. "I hate when you ask me to repeat stuff. It's like you think I'm stupid or something."

"We both know you're not stupid," Karen said. "So why don't *you* tell me why I ask you to repeat some of the things I say."

He groaned. "You think I'm gonna forget, or maybe I'm gonna try to weasel out of it, or something."

"Or something," Karen agreed. Then she smiled. "Go have your lunch."

"Yeah," Aaron said. "And I'll try not to be dead meat," he mumbled as he stepped out of the room.

FIVE

When Ms. Masilo, the music teacher, came to the door on Tuesday afternoon, she told everybody to line up for a concert rehearsal. Aaron lined up with the rest of the class, even though he hated rehearsals. All that standing and singing. Over and over. The same words. The same songs. And Ms. Masilo. She was the other thing about rehearsals Aaron didn't like.

Ms. Masilo's mouth opened wider than any mouth he had ever seen. And she always smiled. At least her lips always smiled. Big. So you could see all her teeth. He found her smile a little scary because it almost never left her face. It made her look happy even when she talked mad. It made her look nice, even when she was being mean.

Ms. Masilo didn't like him either. He could tell. "Aaron, you can go to the library," she always said when she came to pick up the class for choir practice. She said it like she was doing him a favor, but he knew it was because she didn't want to hear him sing. "Somebody sounds like a car in need of a muffler," she said once when he stayed. Then she looked right at him and wrinkled her nose as if something smelled bad. And all the time she kept smiling.

For a long time he was happy to read in the library and miss choir practices, but this year he wanted to be in the concert. Well, not *really*. He didn't want to rehearse and he didn't want to sing, but last week when Gran saw the announcement in the school newsletter for the *Voices of Winter* concert, she said, "Your dad will be here to see that."

"He's gonna come to the concert?" Aaron asked.

"Of course he'll come," Gran said. "He'll be proud to see you on the stage."

And that's why, when Ms. Masilo came to get the class for the rehearsal and said, "Aaron, you can go and read in the library," he said, "I-I don't want to read. I want to be in the concert."

Ms. Masilo's smile never left her face. She stood tall and straight with her head so perfectly balanced on her long neck that she had to look down her nose to see him.

She turned to Mr. Collins. "Perhaps he can stay with you?" she said, as if she hadn't heard.

Mr. Collins looked at Aaron.

"I-I want to be in the concert," Aaron said.

"He-he wants to sing," Tufan mimicked. Some of the kids snickered.

"Enough!" Mr. Collins warned.

"I think you'll be much happier in the library," Ms. Masilo said. "You have no patience for rehearsals. You fidget and annoy people, and you're distracted by everything."

Aaron didn't say anything. His eyes were watching her fingers massage one of the clunky blue beads on her necklace.

"Aaron?" Mr. Collins said.

Aaron glanced at the class. Everybody was watching. He took a breath. "I want to be in the concert," he said for the third time.

Ms. Masilo's hand made a little wave, and she stepped into the hallway. Mr. Collins followed her out. Aaron didn't know if he should follow or not, so he did, in case her wave was meant for him too. He waited behind Mr. Collins.

"I won't have that boy spoiling this concert," Ms. Masilo was saying. Her voice was low, but the sounds Aaron heard were hard and sharp. "I've put in too much work to let him stand in front of an audience and ruin everything with his odd behavior. Who knows what he'll do! Besides, he can't carry a tune."

Aaron saw Mr. Collins tug on his earlobe. "I understand your problem," he said, "but he wants to sing. Help him to sing as best he can."

"I can't make a silk purse out of a sow's ear!" Ms. Masilo sputtered.

Aaron frowned. Silk purse? He didn't get that. What silk purse? And what did she mean about a sow's ear?

He was relieved to hear Mr. Collins say, "I don't think Aaron wants to be a silk purse, so why don't we help him be a really fine pigskin wallet."

The pigskin wallet part didn't make sense either. But Aaron figured if Mr. Collins said it, then it must be a good thing.

Ms. Masilo sniffed. "Not everybody qualifies for sainthood the way you do," she said.

"I'm no saint," Mr. Collins said softly.

"You sure act like one," Ms. Masilo fired back.

Mr. Collins tugged on the same earlobe. "I have a brother who's a lot like Aaron. Things have always been hard for him too. I'm just doing what I can."

He turned then to go back into the classroom but found Aaron standing right behind him. "Oops!" Mr. Collins said. His feet did a funny little dance, and he had to reach for the wall to keep from tripping. He shook his head. "Go back inside, Aaron," he said.

Aaron walked to the end of the line. Ms. Masilo didn't say anything else as she led the class to the gym.

* * *

Ms. Masilo placed Aaron at the very top of the last riser. The height made him feel a little dizzy. When Tufan came to stand beside him, he felt worse.

"There isn't room to stand shoulder to shoulder," Ms. Masilo told the class. "Angle yourselves toward the center."

Everybody shifted. Aaron began to feel locked in by the boy who stood in front of his face, and by Tufan, who stood at his back, close enough that the sound of his raspy breathing filled Aaron's ears. He imagined that breath around his head, warm and moist, rich with the smell of unfamiliar spices. He could see it: a fine cloud settling over him. He closed his eyes.

Ms. Masilo blew into her pitch pipe. She hummed. The class hummed back.

"Watch me now," she said. "Aaron! Are you watching, Aaron?"

Aaron's eyes opened.

"When my hands go up, you take a breath. When my hands come down, you start. I want that first note strong and clear. Together now," she said. Her hands went up. Everybody took a breath. The sound of it filled the room.

"No! No! No!" she shouted from behind her smile. "A silent breath. Take a silent breath. The audience doesn't want to hear you suck air."

Her arms rose. The class took a silent breath, and when her hands came down, they sang:

Christmas is coming

The goose is getting fat,

Please put a penny in an old man's hat.

She stopped them. "We can do better than that," she said, still smiling. "Let's do it again."

They did it four more times before she actually allowed them to sing to the end of the song.

When they finished, her smile grew wider. *As big as tombstones*, Aaron thought as he looked at Ms. Masilo's teeth. That's what his Gran had said when his baby teeth fell out and the new teeth came in. *Your teeth are as big as tombstones*. But then he grew, and his face got bigger and his teeth didn't look so big anymore. He wondered if Ms. Masilo's face was going to grow to match her teeth. She'd have an enormous head if it did.

He imagined Ms. Masilo's head as big as a beach ball. He swayed, picturing the head floating above her body. He saw her teeth standing straight and tall at the end of a row of graves. The images made him giggle.

"Stop laughing, turkey," Tufan hissed.

Aaron jumped. He'd forgotten about Tufan. He glanced back. The sight of Tufan's frowning face made his stomach tighten. He looked away.

Just below the ceiling, pipes ran from one side of the room to the other. They were painted dark blue. Big pipes and little pipes. The big pipes looked big enough to crawl through. Like the pipes in *Star Wars* that suctioned away garbage. He wondered if these pipes suctioned garbage. He began counting the struts that held up the pipes.

"Aaron!" Ms. Masilo called. "Sing after me."

She blew into her pitch pipe and sang: "Christmas is coming," but when he sang it back, it didn't come out right. Even he could tell it was wrong.

The class laughed.

When it was Tufan's turn, his voice went up and down like an elevator. That made everybody laugh all over again.

Now Ms. Masilo will be mad at *him*, Aaron thought. But she wasn't.

"It's all right, Tufan," she said. "Your voice broke. It happens to boys your age."

"It's broken," Aaron said. He laughed. He wasn't sure why he laughed. He knew what it meant from the class lessons about puberty, but everybody else had laughed, so he figured it was all right this time. Besides, the laugh felt good in his chest, and the good feeling made him laugh louder. He kept laughing until a fist jabbed into his back.

"Hey!" he said turning to face Tufan. "Don't!"

"Don't what?"

"Don't...," Aaron started, but he couldn't finish. Maybe he had turned too fast. He felt his stomach lurch and his head wobble. Would it fall off? He swayed. Saw his head falling off his neck, bouncing off the risers like a basketball.

"Uh-oh," he said.

Around him, everything began to spin. It was like he was on one of those playground rides that went round and round, faster and faster, until the world became a blur and you had to hold on to a bar to keep from flying off. His knees felt soft. He reached out, fingers grasping for something, anything that would make his world stand still.

Tufan brushed them away.

With nothing to hold on to, Aaron fell off the back of the riser. *Flying,* he thought as he reached out. *I'm flying.*

It was a short flight, and the landing came with a *BANG* that echoed through the gym.

There were gasps from the class. When the world finally stood still, he looked up into a row of curious faces.

* * *

"Well then," Ms. Masilo said to Mr. Collins. "I'm afraid Aaron was a major problem today. It's a miracle he wasn't seriously hurt. I really can't see how he can be in this concert. I, for one, refuse to be responsible for him."

They were standing in the hallway, Aaron between them. He watched Ms. Masilo's smile stretch across her face as she said, "He fell right off the riser."

Aaron wondered if his falling made her happy.

"Not your best day, Aaron," Mr. Collins said. His brows made a straight line, and Aaron wondered if he was angry too.

There was no time to figure it out, because Ms. Masilo said, "Not his best day! Does he have best days?" She sounded angry, but the smile never left her face.

It never hurts to apologize, Karen had said, so Aaron, hoping Ms. Masilo wasn't as angry as she sounded, said, "I'm sorry. Please let me...I have to...my dad...please."

Mr. Collins must have understood because he said, “All right, Aaron. We’ll work something out.”

“Work out whatever you like,” Ms. Masilo said. “Just as long as you know I refuse to be responsible for what happens.”

SIX

Aaron looked forward to Wednesday afternoons because that's when his class went to the library. The library was Aaron's favorite place in the school. He liked the books and the beanbag chairs. He liked Mrs. Evans, the librarian. She hardly ever yelled at him and, ever since kindergarten, she always let him sit in the same place. Aaron's spot, she called it. "I've saved this spot just for you," she used to say when he was little, and she'd point to the carpet right beside her rocking chair.

That spot was still kept for him, only now Aaron knew why. It was because when he sat someplace else, he didn't always pay attention. Still, he liked that she kept a place just for him.

Mrs. Evans waited for everyone to settle before she said, "I know that your class has started a science unit about space, so I've pulled a collection of myths and legends that explain some of the things we see in the heavens."

Aaron stared at the books displayed on the library table. They had pictures on the covers of ravens and bats, coyotes and bears. One had a four-horse chariot racing across the sun. One had a picture of a boy with wings.

If he had wings, it wouldn't matter if he fell off the risers. He'd soar over Ms. Masilo's head. He'd soar over all the heads in the audience. His dad would point and say, *That's my boy*, and he'd be proud. If he had wings, he'd be able to fly away from Tufan, and Tufan would never be able to catch him. If he had wings, he'd still be different. But good different.

"Can I borrow that one?" he asked, pointing.

"I'm hoping everybody will borrow a book," Mrs. Evans said.

"I want..."

Mrs. Evans placed her hand on his shoulder. "Aaron," she said. "When the lesson's over, I'll listen to what you want. Now it's your turn to pay attention. Your wants will have to wait."

"Aaron can't wait," Tufan snickered.

There were giggles from the class.

"He *can* wait with everyone else," Mrs. Evans said.

Aaron pinched his lips together. *I can. I can. I can so wait*, he said to himself. The words made a song in his head.

I can.

I can.

I can so wait.

I can.

I can.

I can so wait.

His body started swaying to the beat, but that made Mrs. Evans frown, so he stopped.

"I'm hoping that, by reading and listening to myths and legends about the heavens, we can gain an understanding of how early people tried to explain the things they saw in their world," Mrs. Evans said. "And because these myths and legends started off as oral stories, I'm not going to read to you today. Instead, I'm going to tell you one of these tales."

"Is it like story time in the library?" Aaron asked, already forgetting he meant to stay silent. "I used to like 'The Three Billy Goats Gruff.' *Who's that crossing my bridge?*" he said, making his voice deep and scary. "That's the troll talking," he explained. "I like the troll."

Some of the kids snickered.

"That's enough!" Mrs. Evans said. "Not all stories are nursery tales. Why not listen, and judge for yourself."

Her eyes scanned the class, and when she was sure everyone was ready, she began.

"When the world was brand-new, no sun shone in the sky, so of course there was no light from the moon. No stars glimmered in the heavens. The world was covered by a blanket of darkness, and the animals couldn't see. Everywhere they went they had to feel their way, and they were afraid."

As the story unfolded, Aaron forgot to talk. There was something about the teacher's voice that helped him feel the darkness in this early world. He understood why the animals were scared. He could imagine them groping through the darkness. They wanted to find light to bring to their world.

Then Mrs. Evans spoke in a new voice. A quiet voice, soft as a whisper. Aaron strained to hear. "I think I can do that. I think I can bring back the light," the voice said.

That was Grandmother Spider talking. Aaron could tell by the way the story was going that she would be the one to bring back the light. The other animals thought she was too small and too old, but he was sure she could do it. Grandmothers were smart.

His gran knew all kinds of stuff. He leaned forward, listening until Mrs. Evans said, "And that is how Grandmother Spider gave the world fire and light."

For several seconds the class sat silent. "Tell it again," Aaron said.

His words made Mrs. Evans smile.

When it was time to find a book, Aaron chose the one with the flying boy on the cover. "Got it!" he chortled. "Got it." And he clutched it to his chest as he carried it back to class.

* * *

For the rest of the afternoon, Mr. Collins let them finish off work. Aaron hated work periods. They were boring. You just sat and worked. Alone. But with his father coming, he was determined to get everything done to prove he could, and to prove he wasn't as weird as Tufan said.

He started in his chair. After a while he shifted to his knees. Then he moved to sit on the floor. When he finished his spelling paper, he walked to the back of the room to drop it into the marking bin. The margins of his page were tattooed with angry slashes and lightning bolts, and it was slightly soggy where he had chewed away the bottom corner, but it was done.

On his way back he stopped to check out the guppy tank. Then he grabbed his math text and sat under a table at the back of the room to finish that assignment too. His page ended up with three round puncture holes, made when he jabbed his pencil through the paper as he worked out the last problem. But it was finished, and he was sure it was right.

When the final bell rang, he glanced up at the detention board. *My name's not there,* he thought. He was pleased. *From now on I'll finish everything. An' then nobody will think I'm weird. Especially not my dad. He won't.*

* * *

He was sitting on the hallway floor, packing up his belongings when Jeremy hurried by.

"You wanna come to my house?" Aaron called out.

"I've got volleyball practice," Jeremy said as he hurried away.

"Oh. Yeah." Aaron's shoulders sagged. Volleyball. He tightened his lips. He'd put it on the first list: *6. how to play volleyball.*

He leaned over to shove his library book deep into his backpack and was closing the straps when a pair of legs stepped around him. He looked up to see Karima putting on her coat. She smiled, and two dimples formed on her cheeks. He watched her tug on her boots and tie the laces.

Sometimes Jeremy walks Karima home, Aaron thought. *But not today. He can't walk her home today. He's playing volleyball.* Aaron had a new thought. "I can walk you home," he said, turning to Karima.

Karima's face flushed. Two girls beside her started to giggle. "Why?" she asked. "You don't even live near my house."

"Yeah, but I don't mind."

"I can walk home alone," she said.

"Aaron and Karima," one of the girls sang.

"No-o-o!" Aaron said. "No! You've got it all wrong. You don't know anything. It's not Aaron and Karima. It's Jeremy and Karima. Jeremy loves Karima!"

Karima groaned.

"What?" Aaron said. "What?"

She glared at him.

The giggling girls picked up their bags. "Loser," said the first one as she walked by. "Loser," said the second. Karima didn't say anything, but she hurried away, leaving Aaron confused and alone.

SEVEN

After school on Thursday, Aaron sat on the gym bench, watching Mr. Collins and Jeremy turn the long rope for the skipping team practice. It made a sharp smacking sound every time it hit the floor.

"Thirty-one, thirty-two, thirty-three, thirty-four..." Aaron counted under his breath. With each count somebody jumped in, traveled to the other end and jumped out again. *So fast. So fast,* he thought.

"...fifty-seven, fifty-eight, fifty-nine, sixty..." He counted the skippers flowing through the rope. They were laughing, running, jumping, breathing hard. "...eighty-four, eighty-five..." Then, "OOOOOH!"

His voice echoed everyone's disappointment as Reshauna tripped.

"You missed! You missed! You missed a beat!" Aaron called, slapping his knees and laughing.

"Aaron!" Jeremy said. There was disappointment in his voice.

"Better than you can do, Cantwait," Tufan snarled.

Aaron turned his laughter off.

"You know what?" Mr. Collins said to the kids who had been skipping. "That was great! You're all coming along so well that it's hard to believe you've only been skipping for a few weeks. Take the last ten minutes to work with your groups on the skills you want to perfect before we call it a day."

He picked up the long rope and folded it as he came to sit beside Aaron. They were silent for a while. Aaron watched Jeremy coach Tufan on how to do crossovers.

"Pretty impressive stuff," Mr. Collins said.

"Yeah!" Aaron agreed.

"What are you working on?"

Aaron shrugged.

"I know you can skip. I've seen you do it. Why did you stop?"

"I dunno."

"It's hard for you."

"Yeah! And I'm...I'm..."

"You're what?"

"Kinda klutzy."

"Only one way to stop being klutzy."

"Practice?"

"That would help. Doesn't matter what you do, singing or skipping, if you want to do it well, you have to practice. Why did you stop?"

"Nobody wants me in their group."

"Nobody? Didn't I see Karima and Jeremy helping you last week? What happened?"

"Karima got mad."

"Karima? Seems to me she's the kind of girl who needs a really good reason to get mad. What happened?"

"I said...I said Jeremy was in LO-O-OVE with Karima."

"Ooooh," Mr. Collins said, stretching the word so that it came out like a sigh. "I guess that would do it."

"Yeah." Aaron's shoulders drooped, and he pulled in his neck. "I guess it was a loser thing to say."

"Karima's a pretty forgiving girl," Mr. Collins said. "Give her a little time. She might let this pass."

"Yeah," Aaron said again, but he stayed on the bench until the skippers started packing up to go home.

He was reaching for his own coat when Jeremy said, "You coming?"

"Aren't you...? What about Karima?" Aaron asked.

"She's going to the dentist."

"Oh, okay." Aaron tried to sound cool, but inside he felt happy. *I'm walking home with Jeremy*, he thought as he bent to zip up his coat. *I'm walking home with Jeremy.* In his excitement, his fingers stiffened. He fumbled. The zipper jammed. Little mouthfuls of frustration puffed from his lips. When Jeremy started for the door, he followed, leaving his coat open.

"You wanna come over and finish our science project?" he asked when he caught up.

Jeremy shook his head. "Not today." He was leaning into the wind, his hands jammed into his pockets. When he spoke, his words sounded angry. "You know, I'm trying to be your friend, but you have to try a little harder not to be such a jerk. If you laugh at people when they make a mistake, you'll hurt their feelings. They're gonna get mad at you."

"Yeah," Aaron said. "That's what my gran told me. She said, 'Don't laugh at people.' I wasn't laughing at Reshauna, you know."

"Yes, you were. You laughed when she tripped. It wasn't funny."

"I wasn't laughing 'cause it was funny."

"Well, what were you laughing about?"

Aaron couldn't decide if Jeremy looked angry or confused. He wished Karen was here to tell him.

"I was...it was...," he started, hoping to make himself clear. "It was 'cause everybody skipped and skipped, and they looked..." And here he stretched out his hands and moved them from side to side. "They looked like people floating. Like they were dancing on the air. And then the rope stopped and I...it was 'cause it was so pretty and I was sort of happy and..." His voice trailed off.

Jeremy scratched the back of his neck. "Jeez, Aaron," he said, "you're really weird."

"Yeah. I know." Aaron shivered. He crossed his arms across his chest to keep his coat together. "How do I stop? How do I not be weird?"

Jeremy shrugged. "I dunno. You could...Well, for starters you could stop laughing when things aren't funny. And when you laugh, try not to laugh so loud, 'cause people think you're doing a hyena imitation."

Aaron snorted. "A hyena imitation!"

"Like that. That's exactly what I'm talking about. Don't laugh like that if you don't want to sound weird."

"Oh." Aaron turned off his laughter. "Okay."

"And you need to grow up and act your age."

"I don't act my age?"

"I know you're smart and everything, but sometimes when you talk, you sound like you're still in kindergarten."

Aaron's chin dropped to his chest. "I sure do a lot of stuff wrong," he said.

"I can be your friend," Jeremy said, "but I don't want to be your babysitter. You have to start taking care of yourself."

Aaron nodded.

"I'll tell you what my dad used to tell me," Jeremy said. "My dad used to say, 'Look people in the eye when they're talking to you. Listen to what they say. And if you can't think of something smart to say, it's better to shut the heck up.' If you want to stop being weird, remember that and see if it helps."

"I should shut the heck up," Aaron said, his head bobbing as he nodded his agreement. He grinned. "Dads know lots of good stuff. When my dad comes, he'll tell me everything like that too. And when he tells me what I should know, I'll tell you, 'cause you're my friend."

He thought he heard a small groan from Jeremy.

* * *

That evening Aaron made a new list of things to remember for when his dad came back.

How to stop being weird

1. *don't laugh like a hyena*
2. *grow up*
3. *look people in the eye*
4. *shut the heck up*

EIGHT

The sky was blue on Friday morning as Aaron made his way to school, but the air was crisp and cold. Cold enough that each breath made his nose sting. Cold enough that little white clouds of vapor formed each time he exhaled. He lifted his chin and opened his mouth like a goldfish searching for food. Then he puffed. He wanted to make his breath come out in rings. He had seen that once on TV. A man blowing smoke rings.

No rings formed in front of Aaron's face. Just small clouds that hung in the air then faded away. *I'll put it on the list,* he thought. *Dad will know how to blow smoke rings. He'll show me.*

It had rained overnight, and the puddles on the sidewalk were coated with films of ice, some of them clear as window glass, others milky white. He liked the milky ones best. They made a sharp, satisfying *crack* when they shattered under his boots. The others, the clear ones, didn't crack the same way, and when they did, water welled up and over the break.

When he got to school, Aaron looked for Jeremy. He wasn't around, but Tufan was coming through the far gate, head down, hands pulled high inside his sleeves, shoulders hunched against the cold.

"Don't talk to Tufan," Jeremy had said. So Aaron hurried across the pavement and clomped out into the field, where there were lots of iced-over puddles. When he reached the first one, he leaped into its middle, landing on both feet, kangaroo style. Without a kangaroo's tail for balance, his feet slid forward and he fell back. The sudden thud as he landed on his bum made him laugh. He laughed again as he leaped into the middle of the next ice pan. Running, jumping, falling, laughing, Aaron forgot all about Tufan as he crisscrossed the yard. When he saw another wide pan of clear ice he ran, jumped and landed in its middle. That puddle must have been deeper than the others, because his feet stayed under him, but the ice gave way and water geysered up. Icy droplets splattered his face.

He laughed so hard, he hardly heard the voice that said, "Dweeb! Look what you did!"

Still laughing, Aaron turned to find Tufan right beside him. He knew he should get up and walk away, but laugher fizzed and gurgled inside him, like the bubbles in soda pop. He put his hand over his mouth and did his best to keep it bottled up, but when Tufan flicked his fingers at a huge splotch of muddy water on his jacket, it burst out.

"You look like a mud monster," Aaron sputtered. The laughter ended when Tufan shoved him to his knees.

Jumping in the puddle had been fun. Kneeling in it wasn't. Having Tufan's face close to his own wasn't fun either. He couldn't help seeing the dark eyebrows angled over the nose, the mouth turned down.

"That's angry," he said, out loud. "That's an angry look."

"Ya got that right," Tufan snarled, and Aaron realized he was in trouble.

"Sorry," he said quickly. "I'm sorry."

The words didn't help. Tufan pulled his fist back, and he threw two hard punches at Aaron's shoulder. Then, in one quick move, he grabbed an arm and twisted it behind Aaron's back. It all happened so fast, Aaron didn't cry out until Tufan pulled the arm up. Then a squeal of pain escaped his lips. Tufan pulled the arm higher.

"You really do have a death wish, Cantwait," he said in a low voice. "I can't wait to make it come true."

When he pulled the arm up a third time, Aaron shrieked and started to cry.

"Suck," Tufan taunted. "What a baby. You like playing in puddles? Stay in this one. Stay here till hell freezes over, or I'll come back for you." He leaned close. "And remember this. I don't get mad. I get even." Then he walked away.

Aaron stayed where he was, tears streaming down his face, his legs soaking wet and freezing. *My fault*, he thought. *My fault. I should have done like Jeremy said. I should have stayed away from Tufan.*

Ms. Masilo was on yard duty that morning. Aaron saw her come out of the school dressed in her high, shiny black boots, her long black coat and her fur-trimmed hat. He stopped crying and dragged his sleeve across his face. He watched Ms. Masilo make her way down the school steps, one stair at a time, avoiding the ice and the scattered sand. He saw her walk to the edge of the pavement, where she stopped and surveyed the yard.

"Aaron?" she called when she saw him. "What are you doing out there? Get up. Get up at once!"

Aaron squinted. Her lips were wide. Even from a distance, he could see her teeth. She was smiling.

Was she happy? He couldn't tell. He wanted to get up. He hiccupped. His teeth were clacking. He didn't want Ms. Masilo to be mad, but with Tufan's warning fresh in his mind, he stayed where he was. Ms. Masilo clanged the bell. "Get up right now and come here," she shouted.

Several smaller kids gathered, attracted by the bell and the teacher's shouts.

When Aaron didn't move, they started to snicker. Ms. Masilo peered at the expanse of field she'd have to cross to get to him. She glanced at her black leather boots, sighed, and gingerly made her way across, followed by a cluster of curious little kids.

"Get up! Get up right now!" Ms. Masilo said as soon as she reached Aaron. He started to rise, but, remembering Tufan, he sank back.

Ms. Masilo reached down to help him up. The arm she pulled was the same one Tufan had twisted. It still hurt. When she pulled, Aaron yelped and she let go. She looked around, then sent two of the girls into the school for help.

It was Mr. Collins who came running, his coat flapping. "Are you hurt?" he asked when he saw Aaron in the puddle.

Aaron shook his head.

"Then get up and come inside."

Aaron looked at the expression on the teacher's face. *Worried,* he decided. *Mr. Collins looks worried.* It made him sad.

Just then the school buzzer sounded. Ms. Masilo rang the handbell. She glanced at Aaron and started toward the doors. Kids ran to join the lines that disappeared inside. As the last one hurried into the school, Aaron figured it was safe to stand up. He followed Mr. Collins into the building, his pant legs flapping wetly, his boots making sucking sounds with each step.

He was in the nurse's office, wrapped in a blanket, when Jeremy's voice came through the speaker, making the morning announcements. Aaron's shoulders sagged. That's where he was supposed to be. With Jeremy.

When Gran arrived and looked at him, her shoulders sagged too. She shook her head as she handed him dry clothes. "I don't know, Aaron," she said. And then, as if she didn't know what else to say, she repeated her words more slowly. "I...don't...know."

Mr. Collins asked a lot of questions. Aaron didn't answer any of them. He didn't want to admit he'd been playing in the puddles, and he didn't want to tell about the tears in case Mr. Collins thought he was a baby, or worse, a suck.

NINE

That evening Jeremy came over, and the boys went into the basement to work on their space city. They had a collection of small boxes already painted and decorated. As Jeremy got ready to start painting, Aaron stood with his hands in the pockets of his down vest. His mind wasn't on the project.

"Only eight more days," he told Jeremy. "Eight days before my dad comes back."

Jeremy picked up one of the miniature rockets. "What color do you want to paint this one?" he asked.

"Silver, I guess," Aaron said. "My dad…he's gonna bring me a surprise."

"Yeah, you said. Pass me the paintbrush."

Aaron frowned. He handed Jeremy the brush. "How come...how come you don't care that my dad's coming back?"

Jeremy sucked in his bottom lip. He dipped the brush into a small jar and started painting one of the rockets.

"You know what else I put on the list?" Aaron said. "I put *tae kwan do*. We can do that together, my dad and me. Then nobody's gonna push me around. We're gonna do all kinds of stuff together."

A small strangled sound came from Jeremy's throat. He tossed his brush aside. "I gotta go," he said.

Aaron was surprised to see him rush up the stairs. He followed, but by the time he got there, Jeremy was already opening the front door. "You're going?" he asked.

"Yeah. Forgot something. See ya." And Aaron found himself standing in the entrance, alone.

"He left in a hurry," Gran said from the upper hallway.

"He forgot something."

She came down, one stair at a time. When she got to the bottom, she sat on a step and patted the space beside her. "Maybe you forgot something too," she said when Aaron was seated.

"Me? What? What did I forget?"

"Is it possible that in all the excitement of your dad coming home, you forgot Jeremy's father will never be back?"

"What?"

"Think for a minute," Gran said.

Aaron sat. After a bit, his eyes widened. "Oh," he said. "Stupid me. Stupid, stupid me. Should I say sorry?" he asked, his voice sounding small and lost as he tried to figure out how to make things right.

"Can't hurt," Gran said. She sighed, hoisted herself to her feet and plodded into the kitchen.

Aaron stayed slumped on the step. Then he squirmed, slid his hand inside his vest pocket and pulled out the toad nestled there. It squatted in his cupped palm, soft as a handful of pudding. Gran didn't know he had rescued it or that he kept it in a box of dirt under his bed, so of course she didn't know he sometimes carried it around. He didn't want it to be lonely.

He lifted his hand until he was eye to eye with the toad and said, "When my dad comes, he's gonna tell me the right things to say. Then I won't hurt Jeremy's feelings, and we'll stay friends."

He was still sitting on the steps when the phone rang. Gran answered. Aaron held his breath, wondering if it was his dad.

Through all the years he was gone, his dad had called every couple of weeks. He always talked to Gran first. Sometimes she sounded mad. One day she shouted, "Don't ask me again! It's time you stood on your own two feet. I can't support both of you." Aaron wondered why his father needed help to stand up, but when he asked, Gran snapped, "Everybody has to grow up sometime!" and he was afraid to ask again.

Most of the time she didn't get mad, and she almost always handed him the phone when she was done. Then Aaron would press the receiver to his ear and listen to his father say, "Aaron? Are you there, Aaron?"

"Say, 'Hi, Dad,'" Gran would urge, but sometimes he just listened until the voice stopped and the phone clicked, leaving him with the lonely sound of the dial tone.

He always looked forward to hearing from his father, even though they didn't have much to say to each other. And he knew the voice. He was sure about that. For sure he'd recognize it when his father finally came.

Aaron stood up. In the kitchen Gran was still talking, but not to his dad. He could tell.

"Sometimes I feel like a broken record," he heard her say. Then she laughed. "I told Aaron that once and he said, 'What's a record?' and I realized just how old I am."

"Of course I'd like to go," she went on. "I haven't been to the theatre since…oh my goodness, I haven't seen a show since I retired. How long ago is that? Must be nine years now.

"Back then I worried I'd have time on my hands. I thought I'd miss going to the office, and I wondered if I should take up a hobby. Then Liam called because they needed help with the baby. What could I say? Sarah was dying. So I came, and I've been here ever since."

Sarah. Sarah was my mother, Aaron thought. He hardly remembered his mother. Mostly when he thought *mother* he thought of Gran.

"Oh, I don't know, Milly. When would we be back? Six?" She sighed. "I'd better say no. No telling what Aaron will get into if he's left alone."

Aaron squirmed. He didn't like it when Gran talked to other people about him. Not even Milly. Milly was related to Jeremy. That's why Jeremy and his mother lived in Milly's house. Aaron liked her, but still…

"You remember the day I had the doctor's appointment for all those tests?" Gran went on. "I was late coming home, and wouldn't you know it, that was the day Aaron brought home the mealworms from the class science study."

Twenty-three mealworms, five pupae and six beetles. Aaron wanted to correct her, but he didn't because then Gran would know he was listening.

"I have to admit it was my fault too," she said. "He asked for permission. Said he wanted to use them to feed the toad he was keeping in the shed. He loves animals. If it was up to him, the house would be filled with them. He's forever carting home something he found. It's not that I don't want him to have a pet. It's just that..." She sighed. "Well, you know...taking care of Aaron is as much as I can handle.

"Anyway, like a fool I sent a note telling the teacher Aaron could have the mealworms. They're small and quiet, I thought. What could go wrong? Who knew I'd be out when he brought them home! Still, you'd think he would have put them someplace sensible. But oh no. Didn't he dump the whole lot of them into my box of bran flakes!"

Mealworms like bran, Aaron wanted to say, but Gran's voice rose as she said, "You can stop laughing. I didn't think it was the least bit funny. Okay. Maybe it's funny now, but it wasn't then. Do you know what it's like to pour out your breakfast cereal and find mealworms wriggling in your bowl? It took me three days to get my appetite back."

She laughed. Aaron liked the sound. Gran laughing.

She hadn't laughed when she found the mealworms. "That's it!" she had yelled. "You can't keep them! Not the mealworms and not the toad. They're all going!" And she had carried the box of cereal out and poured it on the compost pile in the garden. She made him put the toad into the flower bed behind the house.

There was silence in the kitchen now. When she spoke again, the laughter was gone from her voice. She sounded different as she said, "For all the trouble, I wouldn't trade the last eight years for anything. If nothing else, he gives me a reason to get up in the morning. Still, who knows what will happen when..." Her voice dropped, and he couldn't hear what she said at the end.

"It's all right, Buddy," he told the toad. "When Dad comes, you won't have to hide anymore."

The toad blinked. Then it peed. A brownish liquid puddled in Aaron's hand before it seeped between his fingers and dripped to his shoe. He grunted, shifted the animal to his other hand and wiped his wet palm on his pants before he slid the toad back into his pocket.

"What've you got there?"

He looked up, startled. He hadn't heard Gran hang up the phone, and now she was in the hallway.

"Aaron? What's in your pocket?" she asked again.

He shifted from one foot to the other. "Have to go to the bathroom," he said, starting up the stairs.

"Aaron Waite!" Gran called out in her doomsday voice. "Don't take another step."

He stopped and turned to stare at his grandmother.

"Don't give me that wide-eyed innocent look. I want to know what you've got."

Aaron pulled Buddy out again.

TEN

Right after lunch the next day, Aaron's Big Brother, Paul, arrived with an empty fish tank and a bag of supplies. He draped his jacket on the newel post and blew on his hands to warm them. "It's a good thing you called before you put that toad outside. It's freezing out there. It would have died. The best thing to do is to set up a vivarium and keep it till spring."

Aaron watched Gran's face. She was thinking. He could tell.

Paul looked at her face too. "Toads are quiet and they don't take much care," he said.

Gran threw up her hands. "All right," she said, "keep your toad. Just make sure I'm not going to regret this decision."

"I'm gonna keep it. I'm gonna keep my toad," Aaron sang and bounced until Paul placed a calming hand on his shoulder.

"All right, Aaron, chill," he said.

So Aaron stopped singing, but his body kept making little jerking movements as if a motor somewhere deep inside was running in overdrive.

That morning they turned the empty fish tank into a home for the toad. They filled the bottom with activated charcoal. "To filter the dirt and the air," Paul explained when Aaron asked what it was for. They covered the charcoal with a thick layer of potting soil and placed a shallow dish for water on one side of the tank. On the other, they put in two plants, some flat stones and a piece of bark.

"I think it looks good. What do you think?" Paul asked when they were done.

"It looks great," Aaron crowed. "Can I put him in? Can I?"

"Sure," Paul said.

Aaron placed the toad in the middle of the tank, where it sat, blinking.

Next, they went out to dig in the compost bin. Under the frosty top layer, they found dozens of squiggling worms. Enough worms to feed the toad for a good long time. Aaron scooped up handfuls of dirt and worms and dropped them into a large Mason jar. Back inside, Paul showed him how to use a nail to hammer air holes into the lid. Aaron made twelve of them before he turned the lid over and hammered the sharp edges on the inside flat, just in case the worms came too close to the top. He didn't want them getting scratched on pointy bits of metal.

When they were done, he peered into the vivarium.

"Hey, Buddy," he said. "Are you hungry?" He unscrewed the lid of the worm jar, plunged two fingers into the dirt and scooped out a long, slimy worm, which he dropped in front of the toad.

The toad's eyes shifted. Then...*FLUP!* Its tongue flashed out, and most of the worm disappeared into its large mouth. Only a bit of wriggly tail hung out.

"Did you see? Did you see?" Aaron said. "His tongue was so fast...so fast. Like Jabba the Hutt from *Star Wars*."

As they watched, the toad used both of his four-fingered hands to shove the last bit of worm into its mouth.

"*Bon appétit*!" Aaron giggled as he closed the worm jar again. "*Bon appétit*!"

Before he left, Paul helped Aaron make a new list. They taped it to the wall beside the vivarium.

Caring for the toad

1. *feed twice a day*
2. *fill the water bowl*
3. *mist vivarium with water*
4. *keep the mesh lid on the vivarium*
5. *keep the vivarium out of direct sunlight*
6. *wash your hands after feeding and handling the toad*

When Gran saw the list, she added *with soap and hot water* to the last line.

"Is that cover sturdy enough?" she asked.

"It's just a precaution, really," Paul assured her. "Toads can't jump high. It won't get out."

"I expect you're right," she said. "Still." She turned to Aaron. "You make sure you remember to keep that tank covered and take care of this creature."

"I've been taking care of it."

"Yes," she said. "I suppose you have. Now thank Paul for all the time he's spent with you. If it wasn't for him, I'd never have agreed to let you keep this toad."

Aaron said, "Thank you, Paul." But he was so busy watching his toad, he didn't see Paul leave. What he did see was the toad using its long legs to bury itself in the dirt. It sort of backpedaled with its hind legs, and in no time it was almost completely under the soil. If he hadn't seen it, Aaron might have thought the toad had escaped. But it was there, so well camouflaged that it was hard to see the eyes and the mouth that stuck out just above the ground.

It would be good...it would be so good if I could hide from Tufan like that, Aaron thought.

ELEVEN

When Aaron woke on Sunday morning, everything in his room seemed to be an unusual shade of gray. He lifted his head to peer at the clock on his night table. The red numbers shifted with a soft click as he watched. *6:30*. He groaned.

Outside, the wind wailed. His windows rattled. Something scratched against the panes. Curious, he slipped out of bed and padded across the room. There was a storm outside. The scratching sounds were from all the stuff blowing around. It was white and small and pebbly-looking, more like grains of sand than snow. It filled the air, making the gardens and the houses behind theirs look pale and faded, like crayon drawings washed with white paint. He shivered. Beside him, the curtain swayed, lifted by a wayward draft that slipped through a crack in the window frame.

Snowstorm, he thought. *Snowstorm.* Then his stomach lurched. "Gran," he called, his voice filling with fear as he ran to her room. "Gra-a-a-a-n!"

She was already sitting up when he reached her bed.

"It's snow...it's snow...it's snowing," he gasped. He scrambled across her bed. "What if...what if he can't come?" His body was shaking now. Not with the "I'm cold" kind of shivers, but the scared kind that made his teeth clack.

Gran reached for him. "It's all right," she said. "It's all right." She lifted her blankets to tuck him into the warmth of her bed.

Most times he didn't like to be touched, but this time he hardly noticed Gran's arms holding him close.

"What if he can't? What if?"

"There's still a week to go. A whole week. The snow won't last that long. It never does."

"Six days. He's supposed to come in six days."

"And he will. He'll come. He promised. He'll come."

When he finally settled, Gran slipped out of bed and tucked him in. "Stay here," she said. "It's early. I'll go down and turn up the heat. And you know what?

I'll lay a fire. We can have breakfast in front of the fireplace. We haven't done that for a long time. Today's a perfect day for it."

He heard her steps on the stairs, heard the click as the furnace started, heard the clanging sounds as she opened the screen in front of the fireplace, the thud of a log, and later, water shushing into the kettle.

He closed his eyes, remembering something Gran used to tell him when he was small. "Your dad's heart broke when your mom died, and doctors can't fix a broken heart," she had said. "But it will mend, and one day he'll come back. You'll see. And when he comes, he'll give you a hug and he'll tickle you like this." And she had grabbed him and hugged him and tickled him until he screamed with laughter even as he struggled to get free. Hugs made him feel funny, but he knew Gran liked them, so sometimes he let her hold him until he couldn't stand it anymore.

When he was small, he used to tell himself, *He'll come back. His heart will mend and he'll come back*. But the years passed and his father stayed away, and he began to doubt Gran's story.

From the kitchen came the smell of bread toasting. Outside, the wind was making whistling noises as it rounded the corner of the house. Aaron turned over and pulled his knees to his chest. "Don't snow.

Don't snow. Don't snow," he whispered. He closed his eyes and wished as hard as he could that the snow would stop so his dad could come home again.

Last year he had found a book in the library all about the human body. He read the part about the heart twice. It didn't say anything about hearts breaking, so he asked Mrs. Evans.

"Hearts are not made of glass," the librarian told him. "They don't break into pieces. When people talk about broken hearts, they usually mean that they've lost someone they loved a lot and that makes them feel sad. Why are you asking?"

"I was wondering. How long does it take for a broken heart to get unbroken?"

Mrs. Evans peered at his face, then down at the book in her hand as if it might help her answer his question. "I suppose it's different for everybody," she said.

It made Aaron feel a little better, because he understood that his dad's heart was just taking longer to mend than most. But eight years? His heart had to be mended by now, didn't it?

"Breakfast!" Gran called, and Aaron hurried down. He found hot cereal, toast and tea with lots of milk waiting for him on the coffee table. He settled into the couch beside the fireplace while Gran sat in the big chair opposite. They ate in silence; the only sounds were the wailing wind, the clink of cutlery on the plates and the occasional crackle from the fire.

When he was done, Aaron pulled down the blue quilt that lay draped across the back of the couch and snuggled into its warmth. He loved that quilt. "It was made by your mother's grandmother. Your great-grandmother," Gran had told him. "Your mother treasured it. She'd want you to take good care of it."

And he did. It was the one thing he was never careless about. He remembered being wrapped in the quilt, his mother beside him, reading to him.

Once, he remembered, a stern voice had warned, "Sit still. Be careful. Don't hurt Mommy." He must not have been still enough, because strong hands grabbed him and lifted him away. He remembered his mother starting to cry. Her sobs frightened him. They made him cry too, and his cries turned to screams, as, legs flailing, he was carried from the room.

He was about to ask who had carried him away from his mother when Gran stood up and started piling their dishes onto a tray.

Aaron knew what his parents looked like. There was a picture of them on the side table beside the couch.

He looked at it every so often because he wanted to be sure to recognize his father when he came back. His mother was in that picture too, but she wasn't coming back. She couldn't come back. Nobody who dies comes back. He knew that. That's why Jeremy's father couldn't come back. He was dead too.

He reached over and pulled the picture into his lap to look at it more closely.

In the picture, his mother didn't look dead. In the picture, she was on one of those bicycles with two seats. His father was in the front, and she was in the back. They weren't riding the bicycle. He could tell because their hands were holding on to the grips, but their feet were on the ground. They were smiling.

"You used to look at that all the time when you were little," Gran said as she came back. "And sometimes you'd say, 'Where is me?'"

"What did you tell me?" Aaron wanted to know.

"I said you weren't born yet." She laughed. "I said you were just a twinkle in your father's eye." Aaron didn't understand. Gran often said things that didn't make sense. How could he be a twinkle in his father's eye?

"You look just like her. Same nose, same forehead, same eyes. You're the spitting image of your mother."

She pulled a tissue from her pocket and made loud honking sounds as she blew her nose.

He bent his head to look at the picture. How could he look like his mother when he was a boy and she wasn't? And why didn't he look like his dad? He didn't understand about the spitting part either.

In the middle of the morning Gran said, "I need you to clean the steps and the walkway today. Do you think you can do it?"

"I can do it. I can," Aaron said, surprised that Gran would ask. In the past, she had always shoveled the snow. He'd gone out to help, but mostly he had played while she shoveled. He was pleased that she thought he was old enough to do it on his own. "Of course I can," he said, and he hurried to get dressed.

At first shoveling was fun, and he made plans as he cleaned the snow from the walkway. *When my dad comes, we'll do this together. I'll put it on the list. Things to do with Dad: shovel snow. And build a snow fort. And have a snowball fight. Maybe Paul and Jeremy can come. We could make teams.* But as he worked, the wind began to bite into his face and the sound of the shovel scraping against the sidewalk made his teeth ache. He stopped to look around. Gran was at the window, watching. She smiled and nodded encouragement, so he sighed and went on until he was done.

"You did a great job," she said when he came inside. He felt good. He felt even better when he saw that she had hot chocolate with marshmallows and two cookies waiting for him.

TWELVE

The snow didn't stop falling, but the icy wind stopped howling, and the small, hard pellets became fat, white, fluffy flakes that fell without stopping. On Monday morning, when Aaron looked out, the garden was white.

A blanket of white, he thought. He had read that in a book somewhere. That's what the garden looked like. As if somebody had tossed a blanket over everything. Or like one of those rooms in the movies where all the furniture was covered by sheets because nobody was going to be home for a long time.

A huge maple tree stood in the back neighbor's yard. It looked stark and black and bare, except for the snow that lay on its branches and the mound of leaves near the top.

The leaves were part of a squirrel's nest. Even though the squirrel lived in the neighbor's tree, Aaron thought of it as his.

His squirrel wasn't like all the other squirrels. It was different. It had a flash of white at the end of its black tail that made it easy to recognize.

In the fall he had watched his squirrel chew twigs off the tree, carry them to the top and stash them into a pile in the fork made by three branches. It collected leaves and huge mouthfuls of dry grasses to add to the growing structure. Sometimes he saw his squirrel pop its head out of the top of the nest and look around, just like the periscope of a submarine.

Sometimes his squirrel chased other squirrels that came into its yard.

"Don't fall. Don't fall," Aaron had called out once when he saw his squirrel hanging from a twig. The twig sagged, dragged down by the animal's weight, but the squirrel didn't fall. It dropped to a lower branch, then made a flying leap to the fence. From there it chased the invading squirrel out of its yard.

My squirrel stands up for itself, Aaron thought. *It doesn't let anybody boss it around. Nobody. I'm not gonna let nobody push me around either. I'm not.* Then he sighed, because he knew that wasn't true.

More snow fell. By the time Aaron got to school, everybody was excited.

"Just a reminder, boys and girls," Mr. Ulanni, the principal, announced over the PA system before recess. "There will be no throwing snowballs in the schoolyard. Keep the snow on the ground. Teachers on yard duty, please send anyone caught throwing snowballs to the office."

That day the snow lay deep. It was wet and heavy, and very sticky. In no time, more than a dozen snowballs grew to enormous sizes across the field, each one pushed by five, six, seven kids at a time. Other kids, the ones that weren't pushing, started cheering on their friends, shouting advice and bringing handfuls of snow to pack into cracks and dents to hold the snowballs together and make them evenly round.

Aaron stumbled from one group to another, checking out the progress of each. He watched and laughed, his laughter feeding on the excitement around him.

When the end-of-recess bell rang, nobody wanted to go inside. Handbells clanged as the yard-duty teachers hustled kids toward the building. Aaron was the last one in. Outside, it had been cold and bright. Inside, his glasses fogged up and everything looked dark.

He stopped. He couldn't see a thing. He was groping his way forward when he was bodychecked into the wall. "Huh!" he grunted. "Watch it! That hurt!"

"You wreck our snowball, you die!" a voice hissed.

"I...I never," he started, not sure who he was talking to.

The yard-duty teacher came through the doors. "You'll be late for class, boys," he said. "Better get moving."

"I...," Aaron started. The teacher walked away.

Aaron blinked. There were more footsteps, then silence. It wasn't until his glassed cleared and his eyes adjusted to the light that he realized he was alone. Relieved, he climbed the stairs, but when he reached the upper hallway, he saw Tufan waiting beside the open door. "Today's the day," he said as Aaron approached.

"Today? What day is it?" Aaron asked.

"The day you die."

"I didn't...I didn't touch your snowball."

"But you messed up my jacket when you jumped into your stupid puddle, and I got in trouble. It's gonna cost you. You're gonna pay." Then he walked through the door and pulled it shut, leaving Aaron on the wrong side.

Around noon the snow stopped, but the sky didn't clear. In fact, new clouds moved in. They looked ominously dark, and even before the lunch break was over, it started snowing again. This time, flurries of snow, whipped by winds, were sent eddying in all directions.

At dismissal time, Mr. Ulanni came on the PA to tell everyone to go straight home. Aaron, who was hurrying to put on his hat and coat, noticed Tufan, dressed and ready to go, leaning against the wall as if he was waiting for someone.

Me, Aaron thought. *He's waiting for me. Today's the day.*

He wanted to run. If he was a squirrel, he could run and jump right over Tufan. He'd get away. Maybe he'd even turn on Tufan. Chase *him* away. He glanced up. Tufan was still leaning against the wall. Waiting. Aaron felt sick.

When he saw Jeremy hoist his backpack to his shoulder, he hurried to his side. Tufan wouldn't do anything if Jeremy was there. When Jeremy walked down the hall, Aaron followed. Together they clattered down the stairs. At the bottom, Aaron glanced back. The staircase was empty. Safe, he thought. I won't die today. Not today. But when they stepped out, Jeremy saw Karima near the schoolyard gate. "I gotta go," he said. "See you." And before Aaron could say anything, Jeremy took off, running.

Aaron looked back a second time. He was still alone.

The walk home wasn't easy. At times the wind blew into Aaron's face. He felt it cutting, biting, slicing at his skin. Then it shifted, and he felt himself pushed from behind. That made his heart clench. *Was it...? No. Still safe. Still safe.*

The snow that had built up on the sidewalk during the day was deep enough to reach the top of his boots. Walking was hard. He tried big-stepping over the drifts, lifting his feet high and stomping them down. He wished for wings. *If I had wings, I could fly over everything*, he thought. In spite of the wind and the snow, he climbed a snowbank, lifted his arms and jumped, but the flying part didn't happen. He fell and landed in a heap. It made him laugh. The laughter ended when he thought he heard a voice call his name.

"Aaaaaroooon." It was a low sound. Lower than the wind. He wasn't sure. Did he hear it?

He turned and looked around; the sidewalk was empty.

Then he heard it again. "Aaaaaroooon."

Aaron began to run.

Running was hard, but he kept going until his chest ached and a scratchy *CHROO-CHROO-CHROO* sound came from his lungs. *Like a train*, he thought. The image of an old-fashioned train with a cowcatcher at the front filled his head as his feet plowed through the drifts. The *CHROO-CHROO-CHROO* sounds grew louder. When he couldn't go any farther, he stopped, put his hands on his thighs and leaned forward, gasping. He peered under his arm to see who was behind him. Nobody. There was nobody there. He sighed with relief, then straightened and looked around.

That's when he saw it. A shadow behind a car parked on the other side of the street. It disappeared, only to reappear through the window of the car ahead. The sight of it made him whimper, the sound catching in his throat as he took off again, running.

This time he didn't stop until he reached the walkway to his house. *Home*, he thought. *Home safe*. But with his next step, his foot landed on an icy patch. His arms rose instinctively, whirling, struggling for balance. It did no good. The ground below him vanished, and he fell. Pain, red as a fireball, exploded behind his eyes. He yelped.

Behind him, the voice said, "Gotcha now."

Frantic, Aaron scrambled forward on hands and knees and crawled up the steps to the veranda. At the top he glanced back to see a gray figure on the road behind him: a warrior preparing for battle; a warrior standing, legs apart, packing a snowball, taking his time.

Aaron rushed to the door, but the snowball whomped into the back of his head, making it snap forward, then back. *Ice ball,* he thought as his glasses flew off.

"Bull's-eye!" the warrior shouted. He laughed when Aaron dropped to his knees. "Praying won't help!" the warrior called.

Aaron picked up his glasses, but before he could put them on, a second snowball splattered the wall beside him, sending bits of snow and ice into his face. He squeezed his eyes shut and reached for the knob. When the door opened, he fell inside and scrabbled across the mat into the hallway. He turned then and shoved at the door until he heard the latch click shut.

"You can run, but you can't hide," the voice called. Tufan's voice. He was sure now. Tufan's voice. "I'll get you tomorrow."

Aaron groaned. He pushed his glasses back on his face and sagged against the door. *Tomorrow. Tomorrow. Tomorrow.* The word echoed. *Tomorrow I die.*

THIRTEEN

Aaron crouched on the hallway floor, his face dripping, his glasses fogged. He pulled them off, letting them drop as he blinked water out of his eyes. Then he lifted his hand to rub away the wetness. The movement sent waves of pain shooting to his shoulder and he yelped again.

"Aaron? Is that you, Aaron?" Gran's voice. "I'm in the basement," she called. "I'll be right up."

Leaning against the door, he pushed himself to his feet before he staggered along the hallway and up the stairs to the bathroom.

Once inside, he locked the door and shrugged off his coat. "Ow! Ow! Ow!" he moaned as the weight of the coat slid down his arm. He took a deep breath and gingerly hiked up the sleeve of his sweatshirt. The hurting part seemed to be at the back of his arm, but it was hard to see. He tried looking over his shoulder into the mirror, but the hurting part stayed just out of sight.

I need eyes on the back of my head, he thought, remembering something Gran often said. Her words had always made Aaron giggle as he tried to imagine how hard it would be for 'back of the head' eyes to see through all the hair. Now he wished his head had extra eyes.

"Aaron! Are you upstairs, Aaron?"

He groaned. There was anger in Gran's voice and in the thump of her footsteps as she came up the stairs.

"Do you know where you left your glasses? You left them on the floor beside the front door! And the carpet is soaked. Did you go upstairs wearing your boots? What's the matter with you? Where is your head today?"

Aaron looked into the bathroom mirror. His head was where it always was. He looked down. A puddle was forming on the bathroom tiles.

"Uh-oh," he muttered. He kicked one boot into the space beside the toilet, the other against the cabinet, before he picked them up and dropped them into the bathtub.

"Aaron! Open the door!" Gran ordered.

"I have to go," Aaron called out as he pulled a towel off the rack. He dropped it to the floor and stepped on it, hoping to soak up the water so Gran wouldn't notice.

"Aaron! Open this door!" Gran was shouting now.

"Jeez! Give me a minute!" he called back, giving the floor a last swipe before tossing the towel into the cupboard.

"It...I had an emergency," he called out. "I couldn't wait," he said as he stepped out.

"Where are your boots?" Gran asked.

Aaron pointed to the tub. "I put them in there. I didn't know where else to put them." He did his best to look as if he'd been trying to be helpful.

"Oh, for goodness sake," Gran said. "Pick up your coat and take your boots downstairs to the mat."

She watched as he bent to pick up his belongings. It was a lot to hold with one hand, and when a boot slipped from his fingers, his right hand reached for it instinctively. The pain of it made him yelp again.

* * *

"How did you hurt your arm?" the triage nurse in the emergency department asked. Aaron told her about slipping on the walkway. She nodded and checked the rest of him. Nothing else hurt until she ran her fingers over the back of his head. Then he flinched. "What about this lump?" she asked.

"Lump?" Gran said.

"There's a lump?" Aaron asked. He ran his fingers over a swelling on the back of his head.

"Did your head hit the pavement when you fell?"

"No. Yes. Maybe. I guess."

"That's a lot of answers. Which one would you like to go with?" The nurse smiled, but there was something about her voice that made Aaron nervous.

He squirmed, trying to remember. Had his head hit the sidewalk when he fell? He wasn't sure. He *was* sure about the ice ball. Did that make the bump? Should he tell?

I could rat him out, he thought. *I could tell, and Tufan would be in trouble.* For a moment, the thought of Tufan in trouble felt good. But that thought was followed by a jumble of others: *He'll get mad all over again.* "I don't get mad, I get even." That's what he'd said. But Aaron knew better. He had seen Tufan get mad. And he had seen him get even. *He's done it before. He'll do it again. That's what he'll do. He'll get even all over again.*

"My head hit the pavement when I fell," he said, echoing the nurse's question.

She frowned. "Not sure how that could have happened. The bump is pretty low down. Did you fall on something? Was there something sticking up? A brick? A stone? Did somebody hit you with something?"

"Nobody hit me!" Aaron said.

The nurse frowned. She went to get an ice pack and showed Aaron how to hold it up to the lump. Then she kept asking questions until Gran started to frown and question him too. But no matter what they asked, Aaron kept saying, "Nobody hit me. Nobody."

The waiting room was filled with people. There was an old man in bedroom slippers slumped in a wheelchair; a woman pacing the aisle, crooning to a crying baby; a man cradling an arm wrapped with a bloodstained towel; a girl in tight jeans yelling into the pay phone: "It's not my fault! I was puking all night. What did you want me to do?"

"Sit there," Gran said, pointing Aaron to one of two empty chairs. She stood over him until he was settled before she sat down herself.

"How long do X-rays take?" Aaron asked.

Gran shrugged. "Depends." She peered at him. "Are you feeling dizzy or sick or sleepy or anything?"

"Uh-uh." Aaron started to shake his head, but thought better of it. "It only hurts if I do that."

"Then don't do that," Gran said, and for a moment her worry lines softened and she grinned.

He opened his eyes wide. "Do my pupils look big? The nurse said that if my pupils are delated I might have a concussion."

"Dilated. If your pupils are dilated." She peered at his eyes. "Yours look fine to me. You look a little tired."

"Yeah. I'm tired." He yawned, then giggled when Gran yawned too.

"A concussion," he said. "That's like...that's like a crack in my head, right?"

"Sort of."

"If I have a concussion, will my brains leak out?"

"Stop it. Your brains won't leak out."

"But if I did? If I did have a concussion? Would I be a nut with a crack?"

"You're not a nut."

"I'm different."

"Everybody's different."

Aaron sighed. *Yeah. Mostly not as different as me.*

* * *

"There's a crack in this bone," the doctor said, and he showed Aaron the X-ray of his arm and the broken bone. "We'll put a cast on it. You'll be fine in no time."

He gave Aaron a choice of colors. Aaron picked the white one. "Then everybody can sign it," he said.

"Jeremy and Mr. Collins and my dad. And you, Gran. You can sign it first."

The clock at the nurses' station read eleven thirty by the time they were getting instructions about how to take care of the cast. Aaron leaned on Gran as the nurse's voice droned on. His eyes burned with tiredness.

Behind them, the big emergency doors whooshed open. A gust of cold air came through as paramedics wheeled in a woman wrapped in blankets. She looked old and frail behind the oxygen mask that covered her face. Her skin was as gray as her hair.

The paramedics wheeled the gurney to a spot beside the wall. One took a clipboard and went to talk to the triage nurse. The other stayed, checked the mask, then turned to talk to a man in a green uniform.

The old woman's eyes opened and darted from side to side. She's scared, Aaron thought. Her face looks scared.

Her head turned, and when her frightened eyes found his, he jumped in his seat. It was Tufan's grandmother. He recognized the long gray hair that lay bunched on her pillow. He looked around, expecting to see Tufan nearby. He wasn't there.

The woman's hands fumbled under the restraints that held her to the gurney. She pulled one free and reached out. Aaron got up and walked to her side.

He put out his good hand and felt her tiny, bird-bone fingers close around his. Small as they were, her fingers felt hot and strong as they grasped his hand.

"I got a cast," Aaron said, lifting his right elbow a little. "See. The doctors...they're really nice. They'll take care of you too. They'll make you better." He tried to smile. Her fingers fluttered. She pulled them back.

"Aaron?" Gran called.

"I gotta go," he whispered. "But don't worry. They'll take good care of you."

He was behind Gran, walking toward the exit, when the emergency doors whooshed open. They stepped aside to let a woman rush through. Behind her came Tufan. Aaron saw them hurry toward the gurney. He saw Tufan lean his head toward his grandmother. Her tiny hands reached out and patted his face.

FOURTEEN

When Gran said, "I suppose it wouldn't hurt you to miss one day of school," Aaron sighed in relief. At home, he wouldn't have Tufan to worry about.

For a while he tried working on his space project, but without Jeremy, building a space city wasn't much fun. Besides, even opening the lid of a paint jar was hard with one hand.

"I'm bored," he complained when he went back upstairs. "Why don't we have a television, or…or a game system or a computer? Then I'd have something to do. Everybody else has that stuff."

"Not everybody," Gran said. "We don't."

Aaron huffed. "You never want anything new."

"That's all I need," she said. "Another expensive gadget I don't know how to use."

"You know how to use a TV. We had one before."

"We did. And *you* know why we got rid of it."

He cringed. When they had a TV, Gran had complained because all he wanted to do was sit and watch. She kept making him turn it off. Once she even pulled the fuse, but Aaron, who knew about fuses, put it back. That annoyed her. Then last year, when she found him watching a movie in the middle of the night, she got really mad.

"It's two o'clock in the morning!" she had stormed. "You should be in bed." And on the next garbage day, she asked a neighbor to carry their set to the curb. Out it went, and it was never replaced.

"I was a kid then," he argued. "I didn't know any better. Why can't we get a new one now?"

"It's one less problem for me," Gran said, and she refused to say any more about it.

Aaron stomped into the living room and slumped to the floor in front of the couch. He sat cross-legged and began rocking back and forth as he continued the argument in his head: *My dad. My dad will let me have a* TV. *Probably he'll let me have a computer and an iPod and other stuff too. Dads are better than grandmothers. My dad is.*

His argument went on until he heard a voice from the kitchen radio. The voice was talking about how to make soup. "You can't make soup without onions," it said.

"You can't make soup," Aaron repeated, making the words match the beat of his rocking. Soon he was chanting:

You can't make soup,
You can't make soup,
You can't make soup,
Without ooon-ions.

When Gran came in to call him for lunch, she looked at him and said, "I think you're probably good to go back to school after you eat," and nothing he said changed her mind.

* * *

Everybody noticed the cast as soon as he walked into the classroom. There were a lot of questions. People wanted to know what happened. Everybody except Tufan. He didn't ask anything. And every time Aaron looked his way, Tufan looked down.

That afternoon, Karen called for Aaron. "I was worried about you this morning," she said. "You hardly ever miss school. What happened?"

"I slipped," he said.

Her eyes narrowed. "Really?"

"Yeah. I was running and I slipped."

"You have to be more careful," she said. "Snow and ice can be treacherous."

"Yeah. I could've cracked my head or something."

Karen studied his face.

"What?" he said. Her look was making him nervous.

"I was thinking about something you said last week," she said. "Something about running away so you wouldn't get hurt. Remember?"

Aaron looked away from her probing eyes.

"And you mentioned Tufan. You said he made a mad face at you."

"Yeah." He looked up again. "That was when the snake got out and Mr. Collins said we should look for it, and I found it at the back of the room. Tufan was surprised. And then..." He paused. "Then he made a mad face."

Karen waited. When Aaron couldn't stand the silence a moment longer, he said, "Jeremy said probably Tufan was surprised 'cause I wasn't scared. 'Cause I picked up the snake. He said, 'Probably Tufan is scared of snakes.' Some guys are. And girls. Mostly they don't like snakes. And when I was holding it, I maybe held it too close to Tufan, and he jumped up and his chair fell over. And everybody laughed, and then he was... you know...he was mad."

"Did he threaten to hurt you?"

"I...I didn't say that."

"No, you didn't." She tilted her head and peered at his face. "If he did, and you told me, I'd be able to help."

Aaron looked at Karen. She was small for a grown-up. And she was skinny. Tufan was pretty big. Probably he was stronger than her. Aaron didn't want anything to happen to Karen.

"Okay," he said.

"Okay what?"

"I'm okay."

"Well, good. I'm glad you're okay," Karen said. After a pause, she added, "I want you to know that Tufan is going to start coming to see me too."

"But...but...but," Aaron stuttered, panicked at the thought of sharing Karen with Tufan.

"I'm telling you so you'll know it has nothing to do with you," she said. "You'll both come on your own. And besides, everything you've told me is private between us. I don't share the things I know. Okay?"

Aaron peered at her face. "What does it look like when somebody tells the truth?" he asked.

Karen's face turned pink. "Look at me," she said. "See my face? That's what truth looks like."

Aaron shook his head. "Sometimes I don't get it."

"What don't you get?"

"Like, how come sometimes people smile and they're not happy at all? And sometimes they sound mad, but their face looks all smiley. How come?"

"Hmmmm." Two small lines appeared on Karen's forehead, one on each side of her nose. "That's a good question," she said. "I'd have to say that reading faces isn't a perfect science. It doesn't work exactly the same for everybody. Some people react differently. They might smile when they're nervous or worried, or even scared. It's not something they can help. You just have to know them to tell if they're smiling happy."

Aaron nodded. He was going to watch Ms. Masilo and see if he could tell when she smiled happy.

Karen walked Aaron back to the classroom. As she dropped him off, she asked for Tufan.

"No problem," Mr. Collins said. But it must have been a problem for Tufan, because he stomped all the way to the door, and before he left, he turned his thundercloud face at Aaron. Aaron knew what that meant.

FIFTEEN

For the rest of the afternoon, Aaron watched the door, wondering when Tufan was coming back. *He looked mad when he left*, Aaron thought. Would he be more mad when he came back? The end-of-the-day bell rang, the closing announcements finished and Tufan still wasn't back. Aaron wasn't sure if that was a good thing or not.

As the class got ready to leave, Mr. Collins came to sign his cast. Jeremy and Horace and some of the other kids signed it too. One of them was Karima. When she wrote her name, she drew a happy face instead of a dot over the letter *i* in her name. Aaron hoped that meant she wasn't mad at him anymore.

He was putting his speller into his backpack when he overheard Horace talking to Jeremy. "Our names are on the helper board for Thursday," Horace said. "Mr. Collins wants us to come in early and clean out the fish tank, but I can't. I have to bring my little brother to daycare and pick him up after school. Can you do it without me?"

"I can do it," Aaron jumped in. "I can clean the fish tank."

"You've got a cast," Jeremy said. "You probably shouldn't get it wet."

"I won't get it wet. I'll use my good arm."

Jeremy looked at him. "Yeah. I guess. If you want to," he said. "We have to be here early, like at quarter after eight."

"Okay! No problem," Aaron grinned. He was glad he had come back to school after all. He felt good about the whole afternoon until Mr. Collins said, "Aaron. Your name's on the detention board."

"I have to...I can't stay in," he called out.

Some of the kids snickered.

Mr. Collins said, "I'm still missing your math sheet from yesterday, so unless you have a note, I'd like you to stay until that's done."

Note. Note. Aaron shook his head. "I...I don't have a note," he squeaked, as panic filled his throat. "And...I don't know where it is. The math sheet. I think I lost it."

Mr. Collins shook his head. "Why don't you have a look in your desk and see if it's there."

"I can't...I don't know..."

The dismissal bell rang, its buzz vibrating in his ears. Mr. Collins motioned for the front of the line to go. "You might as well start looking while I walk the class out," he called back as he left.

Aaron bent to look into his desk. It was filled with books and papers.

Math page. Math page. He grabbed the edge of a piece of paper that stuck out and tugged with his good hand. *Stuck.* He tugged harder and tried to wriggle the page out, but as he pulled, he brought down an avalanche of books and papers that mounded on the floor.

Mess. Mess. Big mess. He stared at the pile.

When Mr. Collins came back, he stopped in front of Aaron's desk. *Not a happy look,* Aaron thought. *Not happy.*

"Well," Mr. Collins said, "if we're going to start by housecleaning, we might as well start at the beginning," and he tipped Aaron's desk so that everything inside slid to the floor. Then they started sorting through the pile.

There were three pens, four erasers, two rulers, a pencil sharpener and at least a dozen pencil crayons.

Two copies of the same reader, an atlas, a dictionary, a math text and three binders. There were red, green, blue and yellow folders, a broken protractor, two library books and a collection of papers. There were several wads of tissues (some of them used), pencil shavings, a brown, wizened apple core, and a baggie filled with something that might once have been grapes but now looked gray-green and watery and smelled like vinegar.

"I was looking for those," Aaron said as he pulled the library books from the pile.

"I'm glad you found the library books," Mr. Collins said as he sifted through the mound on the floor. "But what about the rest of this stuff?" He pulled a piece of paper from the pile. "Look. Here's your math sheet, and here's another one just like it. You have two copies, both started, neither one finished. No wonder you ended up having to stay in."

Aaron didn't hear. He was holding the broken piece of the protractor in one hand and scanning the pile. "I had the other half," he said. "Yesterday. I had it yesterday. Where did it go?"

It was almost four o'clock before everything was sorted and back in his desk.

"It's too late to start on that math page now," Mr. Collins said. "I still have a meeting with the principal. Will you be all right to finish it for homework?"

"Yeah," Aaron said. He followed Mr. Collins into the hallway and watched the teacher lock the classroom door, but once he was gone, Aaron slumped to the floor. *Loser. I'm a big loser*, he thought.

The irritating buzz of the four o'clock bell reminded him that he should be getting ready to leave. He began pushing his belongings into his backpack. It wasn't easy with one hand, but he did it, and that made him feel better. Next he dragged his jacket to the floor and wriggled inside. Gran had put an enormous safety pin across the bottom to keep the zipper from opening all the way, and he felt pleased that he could put on the jacket and do it up by himself.

He was on his feet, lining up his boots to step into them, when Tufan came along the hall, his head down. He was walking slowly. Mad or sad? Aaron couldn't tell.

Tufan grabbed his own coat and swung into it. Then he went out of his way to stride past Aaron. Their jackets brushed with a swishing sound. Aaron, who was balancing on one foot, trying to slide the other foot into his boot, wobbled.

"Hey!" he said.

"What?" Tufan said, raising his hands. "I didn't touch you, did I? Did I lay a hand on you?"

Aaron's mouth opened. He wanted to tell Tufan he wasn't going to be pushed around anymore, but no words came.

"You should close your mouth," Tufan said. "You'd look smarter."

"I'm smart. Maybe I can't do everything as fast as some people, but I'm smart," Aaron said. He wobbled again, so he put both feet on the floor before he went on. "Maybe you didn't touch me, but you're a bully anyway. And you're mean. I don't like it when you're mean. When you're mean, I don't even feel sorry for you."

"Sorry? Why should you feel sorry for me?"

Aaron's voice dropped. "'Cause I know your grandmother's sick."

"You don't know nothing," Tufan said, backing Aaron against the wall.

Aaron's heart boomed in his chest. He took a breath. "I know," Aaron said. "I know your grandmother's in the hospital, and I know she's scared."

A sort of hiccupping sound came from Tufan's throat. He stepped back and rubbed his fist across his chin. "You don't talk about my grandmother," he said, but this time he didn't sound all that mean. He hiccupped again, then turned and walked away.

Aaron watched him go, but he didn't think about Tufan for long because, as he started for home, his mind began to fill with happier thoughts. *My friend Jeremy and me...we're gonna clean out the fish tank. And then my dad's coming.* He counted off the days on his fingers. *Wednesday, Thursday, Friday, Saturday. Four days. Four more days. And he's bringing a surprise.*

SIXTEEN

"Aaron, come back!" Gran called on Thursday morning as he opened the front door. Her hand reached out to grab the hood of his jacket before he could step out into the gray November morning. He felt himself being hauled in like a fish on a line.

"Where do you think you're going? There's no reason for you to go to school this early."

"I have to go. Mr. Collins said. He said we have to come early to clean out the fish tank."

"Clean the fish tank? You've only got one hand."

"Jeremy and me. We're gonna do it together."

Gran shook her head. "Look at yourself!" she said. "You look like you just rolled out of bed! You haven't even brushed your hair." Her eyes narrowed. "I'll bet you haven't brushed your teeth either."

Aaron tried to wriggle free, but Gran had a good hold. "You're not wearing any socks!" she scolded. "Did you put on underwear? I bet you forgot that too."

When Aaron didn't answer, she sighed. "I don't know why you think you can clean out a fish tank when you can't get yourself dressed."

Putting her hands on Aaron's shoulders, she turned him so he was facing her. He squirmed, but she held tight. "Look at me," she said. She repeated the words until Aaron stopped wriggling and looked into her face. "You have to dress before you go anywhere. Do you hear me?"

He grunted, and when Gran let him go, he rushed up to his room. Gran's steps followed, slow and heavy. He shoved his door closed. He didn't want her to watch as he pulled off his pants to put on his socks and underwear.

She was in the hallway blocking the way to the stairs when he came out. At the sight of her, he sighed and rushed to the bathroom. With his one good hand, he ran the brush through his hair, then swished his toothbrush across his teeth.

Gran made one of those throat-clearing noises to remind him that she was still there, waiting.

He groaned and grabbed the washcloth draped across the edge of the tub. It was cold and still damp from the night before. It made him shiver when he rubbed it across his face, but he wasn't going to take the time to run the hot-water tap.

"Done," he said as he came out. This time Gran stepped aside and let him go.

"Be careful on your way," she called as he hurried down the stairs.

* * *

When he reached the classroom, Mr. Collins and Jeremy were at the back of the room, Jeremy on a chair beside the fish tank, scooping out guppies with a net.

"Me," said Aaron, dragging a chair over beside Jeremy's. "Let me."

"Watch first," Mr. Collins said. "You can have a turn in a minute." He made Aaron watch Jeremy scoop out a fish and move it to a smaller bowl before he allowed him to take a turn.

Aaron caught his first guppy in one swipe of the net. "Nothing to it," he said with a pleased grin.

"Okay," Mr. Collins said, handing them a small plastic hose. "When all the fish are out, you can use this to make a siphon."

"I can make a siphon," Aaron said.

Mr. Collins's eyebrows rose. "Show me," he said.

Aaron took the hose and pushed the whole thing under the water. A mass of bubbles spread across the top of the tank. "That's the air coming out of the hose," Aaron explained. "And when all the air is out...when it's out, and the hose is full of water, then the water from the tank will come pouring out." He turned to Jeremy. "You hold this end under the water, and I'll take this end out and...ta da!"

Jeremy grabbed for Aaron's hand and turned the end of the hose so that the water pouring from the tank went into the bucket on the floor.

"Good move, Jeremy," Mr. Collins said. "I wouldn't want to explain a flood to the caretaker."

Aaron snorted. "We could fill the whole room. The whole room. We could make a swimming pool."

"Luckily, this aquarium isn't that big," said Mr. Collins as he pulled the hose from the tank. "Finish scooping out the fish. You can siphon out the water when they're all out. Since you know what you're doing, it shouldn't take long. It'll be as easy as falling off a log."

"Falling off a log!" Aaron laughed.

Jeremy nudged him. "It's not that funny," he said.

Aaron stopped laughing, but he repeated Mr. Collins's words. "It'll be like falling off a log. Like falling off a log."

"Are you two going to be all right on your own?" Mr. Collins asked. "I have to see Ms. Masilo for a minute."

"We're good," Jeremy assured him.

"All right then." Mr. Collins walked to his desk for some papers. "See how far you can get. I'll be right back. Just don't make a mess," he said as he left.

As soon as Mr. Collins was gone, Aaron grabbed for the net and swiped it through the tank to catch another guppy. This time the fish in the tank darted to the sides, and no matter how hard he tried, they slipped over, under and around the net. Aaron pushed it behind them in circles, round and round, until the water began to spin and guppies swirled in a miniature whirlpool.

"Cut it out!" Jeremy warned.

Aaron leaned closer to the tank, determined to catch at least one more fish.

"Let me try," Jeremy said reaching for the net. But Aaron wasn't ready to give up yet. Trying to avoid Jeremy's hand, he raised his elbow and jerked it to the side. It hit Jeremy's face with a sharp *thwack!*

"*Owww!*" Jeremy said, clapping his hand over his nose.

Aaron was shocked to see fine threads of blood appear between Jeremy's fingers and flow down the back of his hand. "Sorry. Sorry. Sorry," he said, holding out the net as a peace offering.

Jeremy cupped his hand around his chin and pinched his nose. Then he climbed from the chair and walked to the teacher's desk, where he grabbed a handful of tissues and wadded them to his nose.

"Sorry, Jer," Aaron said again, his voice pleading.

Jeremy grunted. "I should have known not to get too close," he said in a nasally voice. But Aaron could see that the look on his face wasn't happy.

When Mr. Collins came back, Aaron was on the chair holding one end of the hose under water while Jeremy stood on the floor aiming the other into the bucket. His right hand still held bloodstained tissues to his nose. "What happened?" Mr. Collins asked.

"I...I...," Aaron began.

"Nosebleed," Jeremy cut in. "It's okay. I get them all the time."

Mr. Collins frowned, but he didn't ask any more questions. "We'll check the temperature of the water after school," he said. "If it's warm enough, you can put the guppies back then."

* * *

At the end of the day, Mr. Collins was busy getting the class lined up. He didn't see Aaron push a chair to the back of the room. He didn't see him climb up beside the guppy bowl. Jeremy did, and he hurried to stand beside Aaron.

"It'll be easy to catch you this time," Aaron said, talking to the guppies. "Like falling off a log." He picked up the net and scooped out two of the tiny fish. They gasped and flapped as they were lifted from the water.

"Aaron, wait! Mr. Collins has to take the water temperature first," Jeremy said, reaching for the net.

Aaron jerked his arm away. This time Jeremy ducked, but the sudden movement unbalanced Aaron. He wobbled. With the net in his left hand, he needed the one covered by the cast, to hold on to something to keep him from falling. His fingers closed over the edge of the fish tank.

"Don't!" Jeremy said. The warning came too late.

There was a grating sound as the tank scraped along the counter. The water inside sloshed, and a small wave splashed out on the far side, drenching the counter. Aaron's body tipped. He gripped the side of the tank with all his might as it slid to the edge. The second wave washed out, soaking him from the knees down. Then they fell, Aaron and the tank, with an enormous crash, and what felt like a tsunami of water washed over him and Jeremy.

Mr. Collins and the kids who had been putting on their coats in the hallway came streaming back when they heard the noise. They found Aaron sprawled on the floor, dotted with blue aquarium pebbles, and Jeremy on his knees trying to rescue the two guppies in the net.

Mr. Collins bent to lift Aaron free of the shards that littered the floor. "Careful," he said, pointing out pieces of glass to Jeremy. "I don't want you stepping on those."

When it was clear that both boys were unhurt, he ushered the other kids out of the room and called for Mr. Birch, the caretaker.

Mr. Birch came. He looked at the water, the blue pebbles and the shards of glass. He hitched up his pants. "What a mess," he said. He left, and returned with a broom, a mop and a bucket.

Mr. Ulanni came. He stayed well away from the mess on the floor, but he asked questions. When he heard the answers, he frowned at Aaron.

"It's my fault," Mr. Collins said, tugging on his earlobe. "I should have known." But he didn't say what it was he should have known.

Because the boys were wet, they couldn't go home until Gran and Milly came with dry clothes. They were sent to the bathroom, where they went into the cubicles to change.

"Eww!" Aaron said as he stripped. "I'm soaked down to my underwear." His voice echoed in the tile-lined room. "You should see my cast. It's all mucky! I'll have to get another one. You want to sign that one too?" he called.

Jeremy said nothing.

When he was done, Aaron shoved his soggy mound of clothing into a plastic bag and stepped out. He grinned when he saw Jeremy beside the door, holding a bag of his own. "Hey, Jer," he said happily. But when he saw the expression on Jeremy's face, his grin faded.

"I've had it with you!" Jeremy said. "I don't know why I thought we could be friends. You're a loser. We're done. Just remember that. We're done!"

Aaron's mouth made a round *O*, like the guppies did when they were out of the water. He didn't say anything. What could he say?

* * *

That night Aaron couldn't sleep. He lay on his bed listening to the sounds around him: creaks in the walls, windy whispers at his window, mechanical clicks and whirs from the furnace in the basement, Gran snoring softly in her room.

Two more days, he told himself, *two more days and my dad's coming.* But there was no joy in the thought because with it came the worry: *What if he thinks I'm a loser too? Will he say, "We're done," and go away...again? Maybe forever this time.*

SEVENTEEN

On Friday morning Aaron didn't want to go to school, but Gran insisted, so he went. In the classroom, he didn't do much except sit.

Mr. Collins noticed. "Aaron?" he said, talking low. Aaron didn't answer.

"Aaron?" Mr. Collins said again. "Do you want to tell me what's bothering you?"

Aaron felt the teacher's hand on his shoulder. He shrugged it away. When Mr. Collins left, he slipped to the floor and sat under his desk, legs crossed, body swaying. His fingers began picking plaster from the edge of his new cast, the one the doctor had given him last night. There were no names on this one. Not even Gran's.

After a while, the classroom whispers invaded his ears. *Talking about me. Loser me.* He felt eyes watching. When he looked up, the eyes shifted away. Except Jeremy's eyes. His eyes didn't have to shift. He wasn't watching. Aaron knew why. *Done. We're done.* That's what Jeremy had said. *We're done.*

At one point Mr. Collins raised his voice. "Enough!" he shouted, startling the class into silence.

By noon Aaron's fingernails were packed with plaster dust. The one work sheet he had attempted was wrinkled and smudged, the margins filled with slashes and puncture holes. It wasn't finished.

After lunch, Ms. Masilo came to pick up the class for another rehearsal.

"You coming, Aaron?" she asked. He nodded. He walked all the way to the gym beside Mr. Collins. While his teacher settled on a bench at the side of the room, Aaron climbed the stairs to the stage. He stood with the rest of the class, but he felt alone. An island of boy in a sea of kids.

He saw Ms. Masilo's lips move behind her smile, but it was Jeremy's voice that filled his head. *We're done. We're done. We're done.*

When Ms. Masilo's hands went up, the class sang. Aaron heard but didn't join in, and he didn't laugh when

Tufan's voice rose and fell like a yo-yo with a knotted string.

Ms. Masilo tapped her baton. The singing stopped. Aaron watched as she turned her smile at Mr. Collins. "I just had a thought," she said. "Maybe for this one concert, Tufan and...and Aaron could do something else. Instead of singing, I mean."

Mr. Collins frowned. "Like what?"

"Well, maybe they could make the introductions, or they could..." She paused. "They could ask the audience to turn off their cell phones."

Mr. Collins looked at the boys. They stared back at him.

"It's an idea," Mr. Collins said. Then he smiled his own wide smile. "Come with me," he said. "Let's see what we can come up with."

Aaron stayed where he was. He didn't want to come up with anything. Tufan must have had the same thought, because he didn't move either.

"Be cool, guys," Mr. Collins said. "We'll work this out."

At that, Tufan grunted. It was an "I don't believe this" kind of grunt, but he walked off the stage, sweeping Aaron along in front of him. They followed Mr. Collins out of the gym like players cut from the team.

Back in the classroom, the three of them gathered in front of Mr. Collins's computer. Tufan slouched in his chair, his arms folded across his chest, his eyebrows knotted.

Angry, Aaron thought, shifting nervously in his own chair.

"When Ms. Masilo suggested you could introduce the concert, I figured the three of us could come up with something," Mr. Collins said. "What do you think?"

He waited. No one spoke.

"Come on, guys. Three heads are better than one."

Aaron peered at the teacher. He only saw one head.

"We could make a sign," Tufan finally offered.

"We could, but people don't pay much attention to signs. Can we think of something to say?"

"People say poems," Aaron said.

Tufan snorted. "Not me. I don't do poetry."

"Yeah. I don't do poetry either," Aaron said. "Except like...you know...like, *There was a man from Nantucket, whose head was stuck in a bucket...*"

Tufan snorted again. "Your head—"

"A limerick," Mr. Collins interrupted. "That's a thought. Although they're not usually very Christmassy."

"Not like *The Night Before Christmas*," Aaron said.

"Now that's a much better thought. What if you use that as a pattern? You could write an introduction and make the poem a reminder for people to turn off their phones?"

Aaron sat up straighter. He liked things that rhymed.

Mr. Collins tugged on his earlobe. "We could start with something like: 'Twas the night of the concert... and the kids were all thrilled...to go on the stage..." He stopped. "We need a rhyme for *thrilled*."

"Filled," Tufan said.

"Hilled?" said Aaron.

"Hilled?" Tufan sneered. "That's not even a word."

"But we're on the right track," Mr. Collins said. He repeated the words they already had. "'Twas the night of the concert, and the kids were all thrilled / To go on the stage..."

"'Cause the chairs all got filled?" Aaron offered.

"That works," Mr. Collins said. "At least it's a beginning. What do you think?"

Tufan's lips twitched. "There's no way I'm standing up to say some stupid poem. Not unless it's a rap or something."

"A rap! That's a great idea," Mr. Collins said. "You could make the whole poem a kind of rap, just by changing the rhythm." He repeated their words, only this time he tapped out a beat on the desk. When he was done, Tufan was sitting up straighter, and Aaron was grinning.

Mr. Collins typed the words they had into his computer, and after a while they had four lines. They repeated them a few times and made some changes. "There," he finally said. "That's the first verse already."

'Twas the night of the concert. The kids were all thrilled,
To stand on the stage as the chairs quickly filled
With families who talked and moved all around,
But once the show started, there wasn't a sound.

"Cool," Aaron said. "We wrote a poem."

"A verse," Tufan corrected. "We wrote a verse."

"It's a beginning," Mr. Collins said. "Now, do you two think you can work on it together?"

"No way!" Aaron blurted out. He wanted to say the words before Tufan said something like *No way I'm working with this loser*. As it turned out, Tufan didn't say anything.

Mr. Collins looked sad. "If you want to be in the concert, this might be your only hope, Aaron."

Aaron replayed the words *only hope* in his mind. "Yeah," he finally said. "I guess. Okay." And when Tufan didn't object, they got some paper and pencils and moved to a table at the back of the room.

At first Aaron twitched every time Tufan moved. But as they added words, changed lines, counted the meters and struggled to find rhymes, he started to feel a little better.

"What are you working on?" Ms. Masilo wanted to know when she brought the class back from the gym.

"The introduction to the concert you asked for," Mr. Collins said. "It's still in the early stages."

"Can I hear it?" she said.

Mr. Collins asked Aaron to read it, and he did. When he was done, Ms. Masilo was smiling. The smile looked just like all the others, but there was something about her voice that sounded pleased, excited even.

"You could add a chorus," she said. "Something that repeats. The choir could chant that part. And you could add some percussion. A hand drum or tambourine maybe?"

"I'll do the drumming," Tufan said quickly.

"Oh, I don't know," Ms. Masilo said. "That would leave Aaron to do all the talking. He'll never—"

"Yes, I will. I can do it. I can," Aaron interrupted. He looked around, hoping someone would speak up for him.

Nobody did, but Mr. Collins said, "Give us a chance to work on it. We'll see what we can do."

EIGHTEEN

Aaron arrived home to find Gran at the living room window. "You're late," she said when he walked into the house. "I was beginning to worry."

He let his backpack slide from his shoulder and kicked his boots to the mat by the door. "I had to stay in."

"Did you finish all your work?" she asked as she helped him off with his coat.

"Everything. I finished everything." He waited for her praise. It didn't come.

Instead, she said, "Guess what?" Her voice sounded funny. And then she giggled. The sound surprised Aaron. "He's here," she went on. "Your dad. He took an early flight. He's here."

Aaron's mouth opened, but remembering Tufan's words about looking smarter, he closed it again. "Here? You mean...you mean now?"

"Well, almost. He called from the airport when his plane landed, but that was awhile ago, so he should be here any minute." She reached over, pulled off his hat and combed her fingers through his hair. He stood still for that, but when she slid her arm around his shoulder as if she was going to give him a hug, he stepped away.

Dad? His heart filled his chest, banging with a loud, painful throb. *My dad?*

He had expected to feel good when his father came. He had expected to feel excited and happy, but what he felt was...he felt more like...like he couldn't breathe. "I...," he said. "I..." And then he took off running, up the stairs, into his room and straight into his closet. Pulling the door closed behind him, he squeezed himself into a corner, where he sat with his head on his knees, his good arm wrapped around them.

"Aaron!"

He thought he heard Gran call his name behind the *Whoosh! Whoosh! Whoosh!* sounds that filled his ears. He knew where that sound came from. That was the sound of his blood pumping through his veins. It drowned out everything except his worry.

He didn't know how long he sat at the back of the closet, but after a while the door opened and a man's body filled the doorway. He wasn't tall, but he was wide. *Wide as a door*, Aaron thought. He squinted. All the light in the room came from behind him, so the man's face stayed dark, shadowed. "Aaron?" he said.

"Are you? Are you him? Are you my dad?"

The head nodded. "Yeah. I'm your dad." He stood, unmoving, silent.

Aaron knew his father's voice. He could hear it in his head. He had heard it in his sleep. *This is it. This is the voice*, he thought. A wave of relief washed over him.

He waited, remembering Gran's promise: "When your daddy comes, he'll give you a hug, and he'll tickle you like this." She had told him that a million times when he was little, so he was ready, but his father didn't move. Aaron wanted to say, *You can hug me if you want to*, but the shadow stepped away and his father's voice said, "You wanna come out of there now?"

"Okay," Aaron said. But he had been scrunched in the corner of his closet for so long that his right leg had gone to sleep, and when he tried to stand, it began to tingle as if ants were dancing under his skin. He took a step forward, but when he put weight on his leg, it buckled and he lurched to one side. He had to grab for the doorframe to keep from falling. The tingling grew worse. He lifted his foot, bent his knee and shook his leg to make it stop. *I look like a dog getting ready to pee*, he thought. That made him laugh. Having started, he couldn't stop. His laughter grew. It came out in short, high-pitched bursts with snorts every time he had to breathe. *He'll think I'm weird*, Aaron thought. But even that thought couldn't stop the laughter.

His father stood, watching. "Why don't you come downstairs when you're ready," he said. Then he turned and walked out of the room.

It was awhile before the tingling left Aaron's leg and he felt ready to go down.

He stopped on the second step from the top. From there he could see his father's back filling the living room doorway. He could hear Gran. "He's been so excited," she was saying. "He could hardly wait. As soon as you called, he put up a calendar to keep track of the days. You're all he's been talking about."

"He's...he's not what I expected," his father said.

"What did you expect?" Gran snapped.

"I thought...I hoped...He's up there laughing. He sounds like..."

"I know what he sounds like."

"I know. I didn't mean...He's not what I expected," his father said again.

"He is what he is," Gran said. "He's your son and you're his father. He'll need you now if..." Her voice trailed off.

"Liam," a new voice said. "Liam. Give it some time. We all need to give each other time."

Aaron took a step down. The stair creaked. His father turned and looked up. His lips formed a tight, twisted smile. All the way down, Aaron tried to decide: Was his father happy? Sad? Angry? Worried? None of the expressions he had learned from Karen seemed to fit the look on his dad's face.

When he got to the bottom, his father motioned him into the living room. "Aaron," he said, "I promised you a surprise."

There was a woman standing beside Gran's chair. She was tall, taller than his dad, with straight black hair that hung to her shoulders. But the thing Aaron really noticed was her belly. It stuck out in front of her like she'd swallowed a basketball.

"Aaron, meet Sophie," his father said, and he walked over and put his arm around the woman.

This was his surprise? Aaron stared. How was this woman a surprise?

The woman stood with her legs apart, her shoulders back. She wasn't smiling happy, but she wasn't frowning angry either. He thought she looked nice. Except for her belly.

"You're really fat," he said.

Gran gasped. "Aaron!" she said.

But the woman laughed and said, "I sure am. I'm huge." Her hands moved over the bulge in her middle as his father pulled her closer.

"You're growing a baby," Aaron said.

"I am. And it's almost ready to be born. Just two months to go."

"You mean...you mean it'll come out in two months?"

"Yep."

"Oh. Is it...Is it too big for natural childbirth?"

Gran's jaw dropped. "What kind of question is that?" she asked.

"I was reading. In a book. It said some mothers have to have a...a Caesar section, if maybe the baby's head is too big. Is your baby's head too big?"

"This baby will be just fine," the woman said. "And if it needs a Caesarean section, the doctors will take care of it." She smiled at his dad, and he smiled back.

Aaron nodded. "How are you a surprise?" he finally asked.

"It seems that I'm more of a shock than a surprise. Your father should have told both of you about me ages ago." And this time when she looked at his dad, Aaron saw her eyebrows go way up. "Liam?" she said.

"Sophie is my wife," his father said. "She'll be your mother, Aaron."

Aaron looked at Sophie. She did look nice, but he couldn't stop his words. "Gran's my mother," he said.

Sophie smiled. "Yes, she is," she said softly. Aaron decided it was a real smile, so he smiled back. When she came toward him, he stood, ruler straight, and tried not to twitch as her arms reached out and wrapped around his shoulders. He was afraid to move. Should he hug her back? He decided that wouldn't be a good idea. Not with her belly sticking out like that. What if he hugged too hard and squished the baby inside?

NINETEEN

The first thing Aaron showed his dad was the toad. "Can you see it? Can you? It's hiding. You have to look really hard. There. See it?" Aaron pointed out the toad's new hiding spot under the piece of bark.

His dad bent and peered into the vivarium. "Oh, yeah. There it is," he said. "Great camouflage. If you hadn't told me, I don't think I would have noticed him. What does he eat?"

"Worms. Do ya wanna see?" Not waiting for an answer, Aaron opened the worm jar and scooped out a fat worm. It wasn't easy with one hand, but he'd had lots of practice.

"Can you lift the lid of the tank, please," he asked, remembering to use his best manners.

While his dad lifted the screen cover of the vivarium, Aaron dropped in the worm. They both bent to watch.

"M-m-m-m-m. Yummy," his father said, rubbing his own stomach as the worm disappeared into the toad's wide mouth. "Now I'm getting hungry." He laughed. "I wonder what *we're* getting for dinner."

He's making a joke, Aaron thought, so he laughed too. The sound came out as a loud bark. Remembering Jeremy's warning, he swallowed the rest.

"Gran said she'd make spaghetti. She said that used to be your favorite."

"Still is," his dad said as he walked to the door. He stopped there, and Aaron, who was replacing the wire mesh over the toad's home, glanced over and saw him stare at the pages pinned up beside the November calendar.

"Wow! You've got yourself some impressive lists," he said. "I can maybe help you with some of this stuff, but for the rest"—he shrugged—"I'd probably need lessons too."

"That's okay," Aaron said. "We can take lessons. We can learn all that stuff. We can do it together."

The last word sounded so good to him that he repeated it in his head. *Together. Together.* His father didn't say it even once. Aaron hoped he was saying it in his head too.

* * *

It wasn't long before the rich smells of the onions, basil and tomatoes in the simmering spaghetti sauce filled the house.

"Dinner will be ready soon enough," Gran said when they followed their noses into the kitchen. "Sooner if you both stay out of the way. Why don't you go and sit for a while? Sophie's giving me all the help I need."

Aaron followed his father into the living room. He turned on the lamp that stood on the side table, the one with the picture of his mom and dad on the bicycle. Then he perched himself on the couch.

His father didn't seem to notice the picture. He wandered around the room, pausing to look at the books on the shelves. He walked to the mantelpiece, picked up the conch shell, fingered it, put it back; walked to the window, stared out at the snow-covered yard; turned, and looked at Aaron as if he was surprised to find him in the room. Then he came and sat on the opposite side of the couch, the two of them stiff and silent, like strangers in an unfamiliar house.

Aaron looked around for something he could tell his dad. Then he saw it. Up where the wall folded to become the ceiling, he saw a small, cloudy white spot. "Spiders lay their eggs in a sac, like that one," he said, pointing. "It's full of eggs."

"Oh yeah?" his father said.

"Yeah. But I've never seen the spiderlings hatch. Have you? I've always wanted to, but Gran keeps dusting the egg sacs away." He glanced at his father, saw his eyebrows move together. Aaron wasn't sure what that meant, so he stopped talking. The room fell silent again.

They could hear Sophie's voice from the kitchen talking about baby names. "We're still not sure what to call it if it's a boy. We've talked about Matthew, Owen, Alexander, Graham, Brian and Scott. You can't believe all the names we've discussed. Liam says if we can't come up with anything else, we'll have to call it Shoe Box, or Door Knocker."

"That sounds like Liam," Gran said.

There was a clatter of dishes and then more talking. Aaron looked at his father. "Door Knocker," he said. "That's funny. What if you call him Bread Box, or Jelly Bean?"

His dad chuckled, and Aaron felt better. "What if it's a girl? What will you call it then?"

"Then we'll call it Frances, Fran for short, after your grandmother."

"Fran's good," Aaron agreed. He sat, thinking about a question he wanted answered. "Who...who picked my name?" he finally asked.

"Sarah picked it. Your mother. It was her grandfather's name." His dad folded his arms across his chest and leaned forward slightly before he went on. "She loved him. Said he told her all kinds of stories. He was a fisherman. Lived in a little town on the north shore of Nova Scotia. We went down to visit him once, and he took us out on his boat."

"Did I go? Did I go on the boat?"

His father shook his head. "No. It was before you were born. Before Sarah..." His words trailed away.

"Tell me. Tell me a story," Aaron said.

"Maybe later," he said. "It was your mom who was the storyteller. She could spin tales by the hour."

"Did she tell me stories?"

"All the time. The two of you would cuddle up here, on the couch, and she'd tell you all kinds of stories. It was the only time you sat still, when you were listening to her. Then, near the end, she was so tired that even talking was hard for her."

Something clicked in Aaron's memory, as if a missing piece of a jigsaw puzzle was falling into place.

"*You* picked me up and took me away," he said.

"You remember?"

"I cried."

His dad leaned forward. He rested his elbows on his knees and looked at the floor. "You cried," he said. He spoke so softly, he seemed to be talking to himself. "You cried from the moment you were born. You cried all day, every day, and through most of the nights." He began massaging the fingers of his right hand, one by one. "The doctor didn't know what was wrong. He told Sarah to get one of those snuggle bags to keep you close. He said the sound of her heartbeat would keep you calm." He shook his head. "Didn't work. You hated to be carried, hated to be touched, and you screamed even louder."

"I was a bad baby."

"Yeah." The word came out like a sigh. Then his father looked up. "No. No-o-o. I don't think you were bad. But something was bothering you, and we didn't know what. We didn't know how to make things better for you. And Sarah, she was so sick, and she only got worse. She blamed herself. She thought you were sick because of the treatments she got before we knew she was pregnant. I blamed myself. What kind of father...? I should have known. I should have been able..."

He fell silent and sat, as if he was thinking… remembering.

"And then Gran came," Aaron said to help his father along.

"Yeah. We asked her to help, and she came to take care of you. I watched her. She'd sit you on a blanket on the floor and then sing and talk. There was something about her voice. When she talked, you didn't cry nearly as much."

"Is that why you left? 'Cause I was crying all the time?"

For a while Aaron thought his father wasn't going to answer, but after a bit, he said, "When Sarah died, we were afraid to take you to the funeral because you were so restless. Gran stayed home with you. When I came back, I walked in and you were on the floor, right there." He pointed to a spot by the window. "You were playing with some blocks, pretending they were racing cars. You were making car noises. When you looked up and saw me, you began to suck in air until your face went from red to purple. I thought for sure you were going to pass out. Then you started to scream. It was like you were terrified at the sight of me. I thought… I thought…What kind of father am I? One look, and my kid screams."

"And you left."

"I didn't even stop to say goodbye."

"You just took off."

"I just took off." He looked up. "Aaron. I'm sorry. I've been...I'm sorry."

Aaron stared at his father's face as he replayed the words in his mind. *I'm sorry. I'm sorry.*

Karen had said, "It never hurts to say I'm sorry," but his father's face was twisted with pain. Did the words hurt him? Did they make him sad? Aaron felt a stab of fear. What if his heart breaks all over again? With that thought, something closed in Aaron's throat and he couldn't swallow; he couldn't breathe. He coughed, then coughed again. He began making ugly retching sounds. His father leaned forward and whacked Aaron firmly in the middle of his back until he managed to take a breath.

"You okay?" his dad asked.

Aaron nodded.

"You sounded like a cougar trying to cough up a hairball."

Laughter erupted from Aaron. He couldn't help himself. He laughed so hard his eyes grew wet. Then he saw his dad laughing too, and he laughed in relief. When he finally stopped, his father said, "I'm sorry. I hope I didn't hurt you. I had to whack you pretty hard."

"That's okay," Aaron said.

"What's okay?" Gran asked from the doorway. "What are you two up to?"

"Everything's okay," Aaron's father said. He stood and walked to her side. "And everything will be all right," he said more softly as he wrapped his arms around her.

TWENTY

That evening they ate dinner in the dining room. Aaron couldn't remember ever having company or eating in the dining room before. All this time, it had been just him and Gran. She always set the table in the kitchen, and they ate from the kitchen dishes. Today Gran and Sophie pulled out the fancy plates stored in the sideboard.

"They're not mine," Gran explained stiffly when he asked why they'd never used those dishes before. "I didn't feel entitled to use your mother's best china, not without a really good reason."

"Now we have a good reason," Aaron said, bopping his head from side to side. "My dad came back. That's a really, really good reason."

"Yes, it is," Gran said. "And he brought Sophie," she added, smiling at Sophie.

"Yeah. And Sophie...she's the surprise that came with a surprise," Aaron said, pointing at Sophie's belly.

That made everybody laugh, and Aaron's head kept bopping.

When dinner was ready, Gran lit candles and they sat down. *Like a family. Just like a family,* Aaron thought.

"You won't believe how many questions I have," Gran said once everybody was served. "Why don't you start by telling us how you met?"

"I can answer that," Aaron's father jumped in. "The first time I saw Sophie, she was wearing a mask and threatening me with a spear."

"I was not," Sophie sputtered.

"Ha! Were you, or were you not, wearing a mask?" Aaron's dad asked.

"You know I was." She laughed. "I was wearing a surgical mask," she said, turning to Gran, "and the spear was a needle that I was going to use to stitch up the cut in his leg."

"Needle! That needle was this long!" He held his hands an impossible distance apart. Everybody groaned and laughed.

"The needle was this long," Sophie said, measuring out a much shorter length with her thumb and first finger.

"And that cut wasn't all that bad. He didn't need more than a dozen stitches. I've seen much worse. Besides, I don't think he even remembers how bad it was, because as soon as he saw the needle, he passed out!"

"I did not. I only stretched out on the gurney because I didn't want you to think I was looking over your shoulder. I didn't want to make you nervous."

"Liam's always been sensitive to needles," Gran said. "When he was small, we had to hold him down every time he needed a shot. You never heard a boy make such a fuss."

Aaron grinned. He loved hearing all this stuff about his dad and Sophie. He liked that they sounded happy, because if they were happy, they would stay and he would become a part of their happiness.

"How did you hurt your leg?" he asked.

"My leg? Oh, back then I was working on a placer mine just outside of Dawson for a fellow name Herb. I was the odd-job man, running the backhoe and the pumps and the generators."

"Dawson? You mean in the Yukon? Was it a gold mine? Were you mining for gold?"

"That's right. Dawson City. And we *were* mining for gold. Herb had a claim for a small operation. It was just him and me. Anyway, one day we were shut down for repairs. I was working on this long pipe when I heard a snuffling sound behind me. I turned, and there was this grizzly bear coming right at me. He was walking slow, like this—" and here his dad used his hands to demonstrate the bear's pigeon-toed walk. "I'm pretty sure he was eyeing me for dinner. Either that, or he was blind as a bat and couldn't see where he was going, because he walked headfirst into one of the sluice runs. That's like a long metal pipe that's usually filled with water and rocks.

"Anyway, the bear walked right into the pipe, and he hit his head right here," he said, tapping his fist to the middle of his forehead. "It must have hurt, because the bear grunted and lowered his head. Then he whipped it back up, and didn't he whack himself right on the nose! I swear I saw his eyes cross with the pain of it."

"Did the bear attack you? Did it? Is that how you got the cut on your leg?"

"Nah. That bear whacked his head so hard, he scared himself and ran away."

"Then how did you get hurt?"

"I was laughing, slapping my knees and staggering around in relief, and like a fool, I didn't look where I was going either, and I stepped right into the cutting edge of a piece of scrap metal. It sliced through my pants and cut open my leg. So then Herb, he drove me to the nursing station in Dawson, and there was Sophie.

Once she put the needle down and took off her mask, I thought she looked pretty good. Still do," he added with a grin.

Aaron turned to Sophie. "Some of that story's true, Aaron," she said. "The rest of it? Well, that's what we'd call a tall tale. There's a lot of those told up north."

"Tall tale! That's no tall tale. I told the whole thing just like it happened, without a word of a lie!" his father insisted.

"Did you find any gold?" Aaron wanted to know.

"We found a fair bit. Most of the gold from a placer mine comes in tiny grains, smaller than a grain of rice. Sometimes they're as fine as sugar crystals. You have to wash away a lot of sand and gravel to find them. That reminds me." He reached into his pants pocket. "I brought you a souvenir."

The souvenir was a key chain attached to a small, sparkly stone.

"Is that real gold?" Aaron asked.

"Not gold," Sophie explained. "It's iron pyrite, fool's gold. A real nugget with that much gold would cost a fortune, and you probably wouldn't use it for a key chain."

"Fool's gold," Aaron echoed. "It could sure fool me." He held the key chain by the ring and watched the nugget swing and flash in the candlelight.

That evening they sat at the dinner table talking for a long time. When Gran said it was past Aaron's bedtime, he didn't want to go. He opened his mouth to object, but Gran shook her head in warning and he stopped. He didn't want to make a fuss. Not now. Not on the first day his dad was back. But it was hard to leave the room.

Lying in bed was hard too. His room was right above the dining room, so he couldn't help hearing the drone of voices as the adults talked. He wondered what they were talking about. He wondered if maybe, now that he wasn't there to hear, his father was explaining why he'd waited eight years to come home.

* * *

Aaron wasn't sure what woke him. He was going to roll over and go back to sleep when he heard a stifled squeak outside his door, then Gran's voice calling, "Sophie? Is that you? What's wrong?"

The squeak was followed by a heavy *THUD* from the room beside his own, where Sophie and his father were sleeping. "For crying out loud!" his father said.

"What's going on?" Gran called again. Aaron heard her climb out of bed.

"It's all right, Mom," his father called back. "I just tripped over my suitcase." Then: "Sophie? Where are you, Sophie?"

"I'm in the hallway," Sophie called. A light flashed on. "Would you look at that!" she said.

"What on earth!" his father said.

Then Gran called, "AARON!"

"Uh-oh," Aaron said. He sat up. He didn't know what was wrong, but whatever it was, it wasn't good and it was his fault.

He shoved his glasses on his nose and slid out of bed. When his bare feet hit the floor, they mushed into something squishy and wet. It wasn't watery wet. It was cold and squirmy and slimy wet. "Ewww!" he squealed and leaped back into bed just as his door opened. His light was switched on, and when he stopped blinking, everybody was in his doorway, looking in.

"Look at that," his dad said.

"If I wasn't seeing it, I wouldn't believe it," Sophie said.

"Believe it," Gran said. "This is a typical Aaron mess."

Aaron didn't know what to say.

"It's the Great Escape," his father said with a laugh.

"Exodus," said Sophie, and she laughed too.

"It's not funny," Gran grumbled.

Aaron leaned to look down at his floor. "My room is full of worms," he said.

"It certainly is," Gran said.

He looked at the worm jar beside the vivarium. It was open. The lid lay on the dresser where he had left it when he was showing his father the toad. Crawling from the top came a waterfall of worms. Even as he watched, worms slid over the rim and dropped to lie pooled on the dresser. One worm was squirming out from under the wriggling mass, slithering its way to the dresser's edge. Others had dropped to the floor and were stretched full length, moving along as if they were in a cross-country race. Some had already crossed the room and slipped into the dark hallway, where Sophie's bare feet had mashed them on her way to the bathroom.

"Poor worms," she said. "They're trying to go to ground and can't find any."

"You have a list, Aaron," Gran scolded. "You were supposed to follow it so we wouldn't have this problem."

"I did. I did everything on the list," he said. "It doesn't say anything about worms."

Gran huffed, but his father came in and handed him the worm jar, and when Aaron climbed out of bed, they began scooping up the escaping worms.

"This is my fault too," his father said. "I was here. I saw how hard it was for him to open the jar with one hand. I should have helped."

When he heard his father's words, Aaron felt such a surge of happiness that his legs felt wobbly. *I knew it*, he thought. *I knew it. My dad likes toads.* And, for the first time, he was sure his father didn't think he was too weird and that everything was going to work out.

When the worms were back in the jar and the lid was fastened, Sophie went to the bathroom, and when she was done, Aaron and his dad went in to wash their hands and feet. Then they all went back to their beds, and for the rest of the night, Aaron slept well.

TWENTY-ONE

It was Sophie's voice Aaron heard as he came downstairs the next morning.

"This family keeps far too many secrets," she was saying. "You have to tell him. He's old enough to know."

"Can't we just—," Gran started. She stopped when Aaron walked into the kitchen.

"What's the secret?" he asked. There was a smile on his face. He waited for Gran to say, "You're grinning from ear to ear," as she always did when he looked happy, but she didn't. And when he looked around, his smile faded.

Sophie, Gran and his dad were sitting at the table, the breakfast dishes pushed aside. The room was filled with the smell of coffee and slightly burnt toast.

Sophie was holding Gran's hand. They looked…sad? And Gran seemed somehow smaller than usual.

"What? What's the secret?" he asked again.

The grown-ups looked at each other.

"Aaron," Gran said. "Aaron, you need to listen." She motioned him to the empty chair next to hers. There was something in her voice, in her face; he didn't know exactly what, but it sucked away his happiness. "You know how I had all those tests. The medical tests? The ones the doctor sent me for?"

"Yeah?" He sat down.

"There's a problem. Probably it's nothing," she said quickly. "Probably I'm worrying over nothing at all."

"You're sick?"

Gran took a breath. A noisy breath, like a gasp.

He saw Sophie pat Gran's hand. "That's just it, Aaron," Sophie said. "We won't know for sure how serious it is until after the operation."

"Operation? What operation?"

"There's a gland, here in my neck," Gran said, pointing to a spot at the bottom of her throat. "It's called a thyroid. Everybody has one, but there's a problem with mine. All those tests the doctor sent me for showed that there might be some cancer in my thyroid."

Aaron stood up. "Cancer?" He knew the word. Cancer was what killed his mother. "You're going to die?"

"No!" all the grown-ups said at once.

"The doctors are going to look at it to find out what's going on. Probably they'll only need to take a little bit away, and everything will be fine," Gran explained.

"Everything *will* be fine," Sophie echoed. "Even if they have to take out the whole thyroid, there are medicines to replace what it does."

"There are treatments too," his father began.

"You're sick?" Aaron's throat tightened. His eyes blurred.

Gran stood up, reaching for him. "My doctor knows what he's doing. He'll make me better. It won't even take long. I'll be fine. You don't have to worry."

Somewhere in the middle of Gran's speech, Aaron's ears filled with a *THRUM-THRUM-THRUMMING* sound. He saw her lips move, but he didn't hear what she was saying. He didn't want to hear. He raced out of the kitchen and up the stairs. In his bedroom he scrambled into the corner of his closet, where he sat, his chin on his knees, his eyes closed, the blood thrumming in his ears.

It was a long time before the closet door opened and his dad's outline filled the doorway. Aaron didn't want to hear anything his father might say. He wanted to cover both ears, but with the cast on his arm, he couldn't, so he closed his eyes instead. *Can't hear.*

Can't hear. Can't hear, he sang to himself, adding a humming sound to the song in his head.

For a while he was happy that he couldn't hear a thing. Then he had a new thought: What if he didn't hear anything because his father was gone? A stab of worry filled his chest. He stopped humming and began to listen. The room was silent. Aaron opened his eyes. He was relieved to see his dad sitting on the side of the bed. *Still here. Still here*, Aaron thought. He wriggled his way out of the closet and crossed the room.

His father looked up.

"Sorry," Aaron said, remembering Karen's advice. "Sorry."

He peered at his dad, trying to see if the words helped. He couldn't tell. But, for the first time, he noticed that his father looked older than the man in the living-room picture. His brown hair was streaked with gray. Even the stubble on his face was gray. And there were lines on his face. Lines that fanned out beside his eyes and lines that made brackets around his mouth.

"Dad?"

His father's eyes looked into his own. Brown eyes. *Like mine,* Aaron thought. The eyes studied him until Aaron squirmed.

"You do that every time you have a problem?" his father asked.

"What?"

"Run and hide in the closet?"

Aaron let out a breath he didn't know he'd been holding. "Only when...when I'm really scared, I do."

He was afraid his father was going to say, "You're weird," but he didn't. He said, "We all find places to hide when we're scared."

The words confused Aaron. He wanted to ask *What scares you?* and *Where do you go to hide?* but he wasn't sure those were smart things to ask. Remembering Jeremy's advice, he said nothing, just in case.

"Every time I phoned, your Gran told me how smart you are," his father went on. "She said you know things most kids your age don't."

"I'm smart...I'm smart about some stuff."

His father made a throat-clearing noise. "Then you should know that not all cancers are the same. I know your mother died, but we don't have any reason to think Gran will. We'll know more after the operation. But right now we need to make things as easy as we can for her. For that we need your help. D'you think you can help?"

"Help?" Aaron couldn't think of anything he could do, but he nodded and said, "Yeah. I guess. I guess so."

* * *

For the rest of that day and all of the next, they stayed close to home. Aaron led his father around the house to examine things that needed to be replaced or repaired. He was happy to see his dad make lists before they went shopping.

They bought a new runner for the stairs because his father said, "That thing was old before you were born. It's so worn, it's a hazard." They bought a couple of night-lights "in case Sophie meets something else on her way to the bathroom." They bought a whole bunch of other stuff his dad said they'd need. And when he said, "There's nothing you can't buy in the city," Aaron walked a little taller, as if the things for sale in the stores were somehow his doing.

Back at home, his dad showed him how to use a vise grip to change a thing called a washer in the kitchen tap. They put caulking into the space beside Aaron's window to keep the draft from shifting the curtains and more caulking around the bathtub, where the old stuff had come loose. They fixed a cord on the living-room lamp and glued down a loose corner of the kitchen linoleum.

Together they tightened the screws on the hallway railing, changed the batteries in the smoke detectors and tested them all. When his dad climbed through a hole in Gran's bedroom closet, Aaron followed and stood on the ladder's top rung to peer into the dusty space while his father checked the roof for leaks. And, all the time, Aaron listened as his father explained the things he was doing.

The two days passed so quickly that Aaron didn't notice that none of the things they had done was on either one of his lists.

* * *

Late Sunday afternoon Aaron sat at the end of the couch where his dad was stretched out, arms folded behind his head. "Once that cast of yours is gone, you'll be a handy fellow to have around," his father said.

Aaron beamed. No one had ever called him a handy fellow. No one had ever said he'd be good to have around. But his dad...his dad...His father's words filled him with such happiness, he felt as if he might explode, and he couldn't sit still a moment longer. He stood up and began to spin, turning, turning, turning, until the room became a blur.

"Aaron! Aaron! Stop!"

He heard Gran calling, but he was so giddy with joy, he wanted to keep spinning forever.

"Aaron!" his father bellowed.

The sound surprised Aaron. He stopped, but he'd been turning so fast that his head kept spinning and he staggered into the edge of the couch. That made him giggle. He staggered again, this time into Sophie, who bumped into the side table, knocking down the picture of his mom and dad. It was Gran who grabbed his shoulders and held him still.

"I'm sorry. I'm sorry. I'm sorry," Aaron babbled between giggles.

"Sorry's not enough!" his father roared.

Aaron didn't understand. His dad had been happy... he'd said...he'd said...? He wasn't sure what his dad had said anymore. "Not enough?" he asked.

"It's enough for me," Sophie said. "I'm not hurt," she assured everybody. "He couldn't see me. It was an accident. I'm fine. Really."

She righted the picture, then smiled at Aaron, "In fact, I came to ask you to give me a hand in the kitchen," she went on, as if nothing had happened. "It's great to be handy around the house, Aaron, but it doesn't hurt to know how to cook either. Your father's a good cook." She turned her smile at his dad's frowning face before she turned back to Aaron. "Would you like to learn?"

Aaron glanced at Gran, then at his father. They both wore worried expressions. Sophie was the only one that looked happy. He nodded.

"I'm not sure about Aaron using the stove," Gran started.

"I'll keep an eye on him," Sophie said. "I think he'll be fine. I've always believed people are less likely to get into trouble if they know how things work."

"Maybe you're right," Gran said. And later she beamed with pride as she watched Aaron use his good hand to mix tuna and peas into the pasta while Sophie held the pot steady.

When everything was ready, Sophie put the casserole dish on the table and lifted the lid. A cloud of steam escaped, spreading the dinner smells. "Mmmm. Tuna casserole," Aaron said. "My first meal ever. Maybe I can be a chef."

"With all the talk about toads and spiders, I thought you'd rather be a scientist," his dad said.

Aaron's brow wrinkled. He really wasn't sure what he wanted to be. But he wanted to say something that would impress his father. Remembering Mr. Collins's words, he announced in his most grown-up voice, "Some stuff I really like. Like science and cooking. And some stuff I'm not good at. Like singing.

I can't sing, so I'll never be a silk purse. I guess I'll do my best to be a really good pigskin wallet."

He was surprised that his words made his dad sputter and cough.

TWENTY-TWO

On Monday morning Gran insisted that Aaron go to school. "But I want to stay here," he protested.

"You'll need to practice for that concert," Gran reminded him. "Now that your dad has come all this way, you'll want to be able to show him what you can do." Aaron's head drooped, but he stopped complaining and went.

Overnight there had been a change in the weather. The thermometer had climbed well above the freezing point, and the snow, which had been a clean and glistening blanket when it first fell, was now a wet, sloppy mess. At every step his boots sank into slush that reached past his ankles, and water seeped into the footprints he left behind.

In the schoolyard, kids were huddled in bunches, talking, laughing, telling about their weekends. Aaron walked toward a group from his own class. As he came closer, they shifted, and somehow the spaces between them vanished. He walked all the way around the circle. There was no opening for him. He stopped behind Jeremy. "Hey, Jer," he said hopefully.

Jeremy glanced over his shoulder. "Hey, Aaron," he mumbled before he turned back.

Aaron pulled out the key chain and held it up. "You wanna see what my dad brought? See? It's a nugget all the way from a Dawson Creek gold mine."

Heads turned.

"Can I see?" Horace asked.

"Yeah," Aaron said, passing him the key chain. "But I can't lose it, 'cause it has our house key on it."

"I won't lose it," Horace said, examining the key chain. Then he said, "That's not gold, you know. I saw some real gold nuggets at the museum, and they didn't look like this."

"Yeah, I know," Aaron said. "It's not gold. A gold nugget...a real one...with real gold...that would cost a fortune."

"Let me see," Tufan said, grabbing the key chain. "Looks like a rock spray-painted with gold paint."

"Yeah, but it's not," Aaron said. "It's iron pyrite."

"Iron pyrite. That's fool's gold, right?" Horace said.

"Fool's gold for a fool," Tufan snickered.

"Yeah, I know it's fool's gold," Aaron said. "But it came from Dawson. My dad was working at a placer mine up there. He told me all about it. And he told me about this enormous grizzly bear that..."

From inside the building came the electronic buzzing of the morning bell. Teachers rang the hand-bells. The kids from Aaron's room surged toward the doors.

"Hey!" Aaron called in a sudden panic. "I need the key chain. Give it!"

Tufan lobbed the key chain back over his shoulder. It sailed toward Aaron in a high, slow arc. He saw it coming and stretched his good hand to catch it, but the nugget hit his palm, bounced and dropped with a wet plop into the soggy mash of water and snow. He bent, groping for it. By the time he found it, the sleeve of his jacket was soaked and his hand was blue with cold. He sighed. At least he had the key chain.

* * *

At noon he hurried home. He was disappointed to find his father gone. "There's something he needs to buy," Sophie said. "He'll be back soon." But he wasn't.

He didn't come back while they ate lunch or before Aaron left again for school.

"Is he back?" Aaron asked as soon as he walked through the door after school.

"Not yet," Sophie said. "But he will be soon. He will."

Aaron wanted to believe her, but he saw Gran pacing from the kitchen to the living room and back again. Every time she got to the front window, she leaned forward and peered down the street. Then she sighed and walked back again. She was worried. He could tell. Her worry made him think of questions he was afraid to ask. *What if he doesn't come back? What if he thinks I'm just too weird?*

He stood in the hallway, mindlessly picking away at the plaster on his cast, pulling out stray threads and watching Gran pace until Sophie said, "Aaron, come and help mash the potatoes for supper."

Relieved to have a job, he climbed on a chair. Sophie helped him wash his hands. She added milk and butter to the pot before she handed him the potato masher, and he stood smushing potatoes until she laughed and said, "Enough already. I can hear them cry *uncle*." He didn't understand, but he laughed with her because he liked the sound of her laughter. And besides, the laughing made something inside him feel a little better.

"I really could be a chef," he said, dipping a finger to taste the mashed potatoes.

"You'd be great," Sophie said as she tasted the potatoes herself.

Aaron thought about making a list of things he might do when he was grown-up. He could start with scientist and chef and add pilot and astronaut, 'cause then he'd really be able to fly. And maybe gold mining. If he was a gold miner, he might find real gold and be rich. While he was trying to think of what else to add, his dad walked through the door.

"Where have you been?" Gran asked.

His father looked surprised. "I was shopping. I told you, there's something I wanted to buy."

"Did you get it?" Aaron asked.

His father hung up his coat before he answered. "No." He sounded tired. "I went from store to store, but when all was said and done, I couldn't make up my mind. That's what you get in the big city. Too many stores, too many choices. I finally decided to sleep on it." He went on then to talk about how much things had changed since he had left Toronto. But Aaron was stuck with the thought that maybe his father didn't like big-city stores after all.

TWENTY-THREE

On Tuesday morning Aaron *really* didn't want to go to school. He wanted to be with Gran. In case. But a taxi had come early, before he was dressed, and Gran and his dad had climbed in. Aaron had watched them drive away.

"It's not fair. It's not fair. I wanted to go. I wanted to go," he complained to Sophie.

"I know," she said.

"What if...what if...?"

"Don't think those thoughts," she said, placing her hand on his shoulder. He twitched. He didn't want her comfort. Not today.

"Sorry," she said, taking the hand away. "But just so you know, I think your gran is right. Your place is at school. Sitting in a hospital waiting room is a long, boring way to spend your time. Besides, your dad said he'd call as soon as he knew anything. And as soon as I hear, I'll let you know. I promise. I'll let you know."

So Aaron went.

Talk about a long, boring way to spend your time, he thought as the morning dragged on. There were lessons in spelling and fractions and how to use quotation marks.

"Are you with us, Aaron?" Mr. Collins asked several times. Every time he heard his name, Aaron looked at Mr. Collins and nodded, but all the time he was thinking about Sophie. When was she going to let him know?

Just before recess, Mr. Ulanni announced that it was too wet to go outside. Kids cheered and pulled out cards and board games. They paired up and began to play. Except Aaron. He sat in his chair, waiting.

Some time before noon, Mr. Collins asked the class to take out their journals and write about their weekend. Aaron thought about all the things he could write about—his gran being sick, his dad coming home, the bear story, Sophie, the new baby—but his ideas jumbled together in his mind and he couldn't decide which one to tell.

Something inside him was beginning to run faster and faster. It made his brain feel a little woozy. He stood up and walked to the back of the room and checked out the fish. He peered at the snake and the turtles. Then he slipped to the floor and crawled under a table, where he turned round and round on the spot, until everything outside became as blurry as his insides. When he stopped, he closed his eyes and sat humming softly and rocking. He was so busy humming and rocking that he didn't hear anything except the sounds in his head, until someone started calling his name. He heard, but he wasn't sure if the sound was coming from the inside or the outside of his head.

Karima's face appeared. She was on her hands and knees, facing him. "Aaron," she said.

He stared. Karima was wearing a hair band. It was gold with a black stripe. *Iron pyrite*, he thought. *It looks just like iron pyrite.*

"Aaron? Did you hear me?"

"Yeah?"

"Mr. Ulanni wants to talk to you."

"Uh-huh," he said, but his mind was on the hair band.

"He's at the door, Aaron. He's waiting for you." She reached for his hand. He pulled away.

"Aaron. The principal is waiting," she said again.

He stretched his neck and looked out from under the table. When he saw Mr. Ulanni in the doorway, he crawled out and walked over to him.

"You need to come with me," Mr. Ulanni said. He turned to Mr. Collins. "Perhaps you could come too. I'll ask Mrs. Evans to cover your class for a few minutes."

So the three of them, Mr. Ulanni, Mr. Collins and Aaron, walked side by side along the hall, down the stairs and toward the school office.

Aaron glanced at the adults, one on each side of him. Neither one of them spoke. *This is bad*, Aaron thought. *Bad. Bad. Bad. Death march. Firing squad. Doomed to die.*

He'd been called to the principal's office before, but he'd never been picked up by the principal himself or marched down by two grown-ups.

In the office, Mr. Ulanni pointed him to a chair inside his private room. "Sit down, Aaron," he said. "We'll be right with you." Then he closed the door but stayed outside talking to Mr. Collins.

Aaron strained to hear. They had to be talking about him. What were they saying? Had he done something wrong? He tried to remember. He'd been in the principal's office often enough to know that the chairs were too high and too wide for him. He knew if his back lined up with the back of the chair, his feet would stick up and make him look like a little kid. So he anchored his feet to the floor and perched on the front edge.

When the door opened, Mr. Ulanni came in and sat down behind his desk. "I have a message for you," he said.

A sort of sick feeling washed over Aaron. "It's Gran, isn't it? Is she...is she...?"

Mr. Ulanni's eyebrows made a knot over his nose as he peered at a piece of paper. "According to Sophie, your gran is fine. Do you know Sophie?"

"Of course I know Sophie. She came with my dad. She was the surprise. And she came with a surprise. It's a baby. That's *her* surprise. A baby. They're just not sure what to call it. If it's a boy, that is. If it's a girl, they're going to call it Fran, like my gran. My gran Fran. That rhymes, doesn't it? Just like the poem we're writing for the concert. It rhymes too."

"Aaron." Mr. Ulanni leaned forward. "Aaron, look at me."

Aaron stopped talking. He leaned forward, elbows on his knees and stared into the principal's face.

"Sophie told me part of your gran's thyroid had to be removed, but she will be fine. Do you understand any of that?"

Aaron nodded. "Yeah. It means she's not going to die. She isn't going to die, right?"

"Right. But there seems to be a small problem with Sophie, which is why she called."

"Did she have the baby? Did they have to...? Did they do one of those Caesar sections?"

"Aaron! No! Your dad's still at the hospital with your grandmother. Sophie wanted to come and tell you Gran's good news herself, but while she was on her way here, she slipped on the sidewalk."

"It's very slippery out there," Aaron said.

"Yes. It certainly is. Anyway, a taxi took Sophie to the hospital to be checked out. She said it's only a precaution. She said she was fine, but she was worried you won't have anyplace to go at noon. She wanted us to find a neighbor's or a friend's house you can go to, until someone in your family comes home."

For what seemed a long time, Aaron sat. Then he said, "I can go home alone. I know how to cook. I can make tuna casserole. Sophie showed me."

"That's great," Mr. Ulanni said. "But Sophie specifically asked that we find someplace you could go."

"Oh. Okay. Where should I go?"

Mr. Ulanni shifted in his chair. He looked relieved when his door opened and Mr. Collins came in.

"I've just phoned Jeremy's home, Aaron," Mr. Collins explained. "And Milly said you should come home with him."

"Jeremy?"

"You two are friends, right? Milly said she'd make your lunch, and dinner if you need it. Are you okay with that?"

Aaron nodded. "I'm okay with that," he said. But his shoulders sagged as he spoke, because he knew Jeremy wouldn't be.

TWENTY-FOUR

At noon Aaron trailed behind Jeremy through the slush and sidewalk puddles. He noticed Jeremy kept his head down the whole way and didn't say anything. Nothing. Not one word. He didn't even look back. Aaron knew what that meant. Jeremy had said they were done, and he had meant it. They were done. They couldn't be friends. Not anymore. Not since they were done.

He felt a little better when Milly smiled and welcomed him in. She had lunch waiting for them. It was vegetable soup and a grilled cheese sandwich. Jeremy spooned in the soup and wolfed down his sandwich. He hardly talked to Milly, and he didn't talk to Aaron at all. When he was done, he excused himself from the table and went into the living room to watch television. Milly frowned as she watched him go, but she stayed in the kitchen with Aaron.

He was staring at the soup in his bowl. Vegetable soup. He hated vegetable soup. It was because of all the lumps. They were different shapes and sizes and colors. He didn't like soup when he couldn't see what was inside. And now all these mystery bits were floating around like bumper cars. He poked his spoon at something green. It disappeared into the orange broth.

"I see vegetable soup is not your thing," Milly said. "Leave it if you don't like it. I'll pour you a glass of milk."

Aaron looked up gratefully, then started on his sandwich. Between bites, he answered Milly's questions about Gran, about his dad and Sophie, about school and other stuff. When he was finished, she collected the dishes. "Why don't you see if you can talk to Jeremy," she said. "He seems to be having an off day."

In the living room Jeremy lay sprawled across a large chair. He was frowning. Aaron remembered Karen warning him not to annoy somebody who was frowning. He remembered Jeremy telling him to be quiet unless he had something smart to say. He knew there was all kinds of stuff he *shouldn't* do, but he had no idea what he *should* do. He leaned against the doorjamb and watched TV from there.

What he saw made him frown. In the movie Jeremy was watching, a mammoth and a saber-toothed tiger were walking side by side. "That's not possible," he said, forgetting that he meant to stay silent. "Saber-toothed tigers and mammoths were enemies."

Jeremy said nothing.

A new animal appeared. The new animal had a mouthful of teeth. It was clumsy and silly and it talked—a lot. It made the saber-toothed tiger and the mammoth roll their eyes. Karen had told him what that meant, but the new animal didn't know any better, and it kept talking.

"They think he's a pest," Aaron said, "'cause he talks all the time."

"You think?" Jeremy said.

"Yeah. And maybe they don't want him around, 'cause he doesn't know how to shut the heck up. Maybe..." Aaron stopped. On the TV, the annoying animal was still talking. *Like me,* he thought. *He's like me.*

"Are they gonna tell him to get lost?" he asked.

"What?"

"'Cause he does everything wrong and he never shuts up. Will they stop being his friend?"

"Nah. They make up in the end. It's a movie."

"Not like in real life, huh? In real life they'd say 'We're done,' and they wouldn't be friends anymore."

Aaron's words brought a flush to Jeremy's face. "For crying out loud!" Jeremy said. "You're really bugging me! Not only do you have to come home with me, but now you won't shut up and leave me alone. Don't you ever stop? You're a real pain! Why can't you sit down and be quiet!"

Surprised by Jeremy's words, Aaron plopped to the floor. It was as if a hole opened under his feet and he fell in. He was standing one second, sitting the next. If Jeremy wanted him to sit, he'd sit. He'd be quiet. He'd do whatever it took to make Jeremy change his mind and be his friend again.

When he looked up, Jeremy was staring at him, eyes wide. One side of his mouth began to twitch. That turned into a smile, and to Aaron's surprise, Jeremy burst out laughing.

"What? What's so funny?"

"You are." Jeremy sighed. "You made me remember the day my dad and I went fishing."

"Fishing?" Aaron didn't get it.

"We were on the river in this old rowboat, and I got a bite and stood up to reel it in. I wobbled, sort of like you did when you were on the chair beside the fish tank. That made the boat tilt. My dad stood up and grabbed for me, but I dropped straight down just like you did, so he was the one who lost his balance and fell overboard."

"Was he mad?"

"That's just it. I thought he would be, 'cause I sure felt like a loser for doing something so stupid."

"What did he say?"

"He said, 'If everything goes smoothly all the time, we'll never have good stories to tell.'"

Aaron frowned. "I don't get it."

"You and the fish tank...I just realized I'll be able to tell that story the same way my dad told about falling into the river."

"So from now on, you won't get mad when I do something wrong?"

"I will so! Don't be doing stuff on purpose."

For a little while Aaron said nothing. Then: "Your dad, he was a really smart guy."

"Yeah..." Jeremy took a breath. Then he said, "You're lucky. Your dad came back."

"I know."

"Is he nice?"

"Yeah. But maybe he thinks I'm a little weird."

"Well, you are," Jeremy said.

"I know."

They walked back to school together.

TWENTY-FIVE

Mr. Collins turned off the video camera. "That's a wrap," he said.

"Finally!" Aaron sighed. Mr. Collins had made them rehearse their poem in a different place every day. Once he had Aaron say the poem while he climbed up and down the hallway stairs. Tufan got to sit at the bottom to play his drum, so he didn't mind, but it was exhausting for Aaron.

Other times he had Aaron repeat the poem while he ran laps or bounced a ball. Tufan would have been happy to do any of those things, but they were hard for Aaron. Still, he got to the point where he could say the words no matter what else he was doing.

That's when Mr. Collins explained about adding pauses and using his voice to make the words more interesting. And today he had set up a video camera.

"You're still talking too fast," Tufan said as they replayed the film.

"Yeah," Aaron said, "and sometimes I forget to stand still."

"Sometimes?" Tufan snickered.

"Not to worry," Mr. Collins cut in. "I have an idea that may help."

There was a knock on the door.

They all turned. "Who the heck is that?" Tufan mumbled, but Aaron hurried across the room. "Hey, Dad!" he said. "What are you doing here?"

"Your gran's been asking for you. I told her I'd come by and pick you up." He turned to Mr. Collins, who had followed Aaron to the door. "Is that all right?"

"Of course." The teacher put out his hand. "Dave Collins," he said.

"Liam Waite," Aaron's dad said. They shook. Aaron beamed.

"See you on Thursday," Mr. Collins said as they were leaving.

Aaron's father paused. "Thursday?"

"The concert," Aaron explained. "I'm going to be in it this year. For you. And Sophie. Sophie can come too."

"Thursday," his dad said again. "Well, that's great. We'll be here."

* * *

As it was, they didn't go to see Gran right away, and by the time they got to the hospital, Aaron was exploding with news.

"Guess what!" he said as they walked into her room. "Yesterday when Dad was out, he was shopping for a computer and a printer and a webcam. And today we bought it. Tonight we're gonna set it all up. And I know how to use everything. I do. I learned how at school. Except the webcam. I don't know how to use that. But Dad's gonna show me. When you come home, I can show you."

He saw Gran smile at his dad. "So that's what kept you so long," she said. "I was afraid..."

"Yeah. I know. But I told you. That's never gonna happen again. I've got too much to lose."

Aaron didn't understand what they were talking about. He was going to ask, but Gran turned to him and said, "It may surprise you to know that after thirty-two years in an office, I know how to use a computer." Her voice sounded different. Kind of rough and papery.

He pointed at the bandage around her throat. "Does it hurt?" he asked instead.

"Hardly at all," she rasped. "I can come home the day after tomorrow." She turned to his dad. "Liam? What about Sophie? How is she?"

"She's fine. The doctor checked her out. He said pregnant women don't balance all that well, but they're not as fragile as they look. She's back at the house, lying down, but she's fine."

"Does that mean...?" Lines folded across Gran's brow.

"It means that everything can go on as planned."

"What's planned?" Aaron asked.

"We'll go out for dinner, just you and me," his dad said. "We'll have a man-to-man talk and I'll fill you in."

Gran's brow wrinkled again. "Maybe you should wait until I get home."

"No!" Aaron said. "I'm ready for a man-to-man. I am."

After that he was eager to leave. His dad was going to fill him in. They would talk. Man-to-man.

But when he turned to wave goodbye and saw Gran's face twitch into a smile, he wavered, part of him yearning to stay with her, the other part eager to go with his dad.

* * *

They were seated opposite each other at the pizza place Aaron had chosen for dinner. Now that they were here, he wasn't all that hungry. It was a little noisy. There were three boys about Paul's age at the corner table, talking and laughing.

"I'm famished," his father said, biting into a large slice overflowing with pepperoni and vegetables.

Aaron stared at his slice. He only liked cheese on his pizza. All this other stuff—he grimaced and picked off a slice of tomato, some olives and onions. His father didn't seem to notice, and he finished his first piece before Aaron even took a bite.

"I hope you know that Sophie really likes you," his dad said between bites of his second slice. "I was so relieved. I wasn't sure what would happen if she didn't. Or if you didn't like her. I was pretty sure you'd like her. She's amazing, isn't she? You do like her, don't you?"

"Sophie's cool!" Aaron said. He was doing his best to pay attention. He wanted to get this man-to-man talk right.

His dad wiped a serviette into the corners of his mouth. "It's such a relief that your gran's going to be all right," he said. "I wasn't sure how things would go if she wasn't. Now we won't have to worry when we go back to Dawson."

In the kitchen, a man pulled a fresh pizza from the oven. One of the boys at the corner table smacked his palm on the table. "No way!" he said. The other boys laughed.

Aaron blinked. He replayed his father's words. *When* we *go back to Dawson.* Is that what he said? *When* we *go back to Dawson.*

"Dawson?" Aaron said.

"After next week. Your gran will be able to manage by then. Milly has offered to come by and help out with the groceries and laundry if she needs it. I think we've got everything covered. She's a pretty feisty lady, your gran."

Aaron pulled an anchovy from his pizza. *Dawson?* "You mean, Gran's not going?" he asked.

"To Dawson? Of course not. She lives here."

"But...you came home."

"Because I was worried. That word *cancer* gives me the shivers."

Aaron's brow wrinkled. This man-to-man talk was confusing.

"You came for Gran?"

"Well, and you too, of course."

Me too. He came for me. We're going home to Dawson? Gran's not?

His dad took another bite. Chewed. Drank some water. "I haven't seen you since...well...not for a long time," he said. "And I felt pretty bad about leaving like that. You get that, don't you?"

Aaron nodded. He thought he understood. Then one of the boys in the corner shouted, "You lie! That's not it at all!" The other boys laughed, and Aaron realized he didn't understand anything. He peered at his father.

"Everything is working out," his dad was saying. "Sophie got to meet you. And, like I said, it's great that she likes you." He took a big drink of water, wiped his mouth, looked at his watch. "Eat up, Aaron," he said. "We still have a lot to do."

Aaron nibbled at the crust of his pizza. He chewed, swallowed and took a drink from his own water before he had the courage to ask, "And you? Do you like me?"

"Hey! You're my kid. Of course I like you."

"'Cause I'm your kid?" Aaron paused. "I'm not..." The words he wanted to say were sticking in his throat. He tried again. "You said I'm not what you expected."

"Oh. You heard that."

Aaron nodded. "I know I'm weird. Even Jeremy says I'm weird, and he's my friend."

"Hey! You're not that…" His father stopped. His hands had been folding his serviette into a small square. Now he opened it, smoothed it, then scrunched it into his fist before he let it drop to the table.

Aaron looked at the mashed serviette. "Yeah," he said. "I'm not."

There was more laughter from the boys at the corner table.

* * *

That evening Aaron didn't know what to do with himself. His dad was busy setting up the computer in the little alcove in the upstairs hallway. "Step aside," he told Aaron as he bent to plug cords into the hard drive and the printer.

Aaron took a step back. His father had been working ever since they came back from the restaurant. And ever since he had started unpacking, he had been saying things like, "Don't touch that."

"You're in my light."

"Watch it, you'll break that."

"Just leave that."

Aaron was confused. Where was the dad who told him he was a handy fellow? The dad who let him help with all those house repairs?

"Don't touch that," his father warned again as Aaron unfolded a cord. Aaron dropped it to the floor and went downstairs to where Sophie was sitting on the couch beside the fire, the blue quilt across her lap.

"That's mine," he said, lifting his chin toward the quilt.

"Do you mind sharing?"

Aaron plonked himself down beside her, then sat, ruler straight, as she spread the quilt so that it covered both their knees. For a while they stayed silent and he stared at the flames, but in his mind an argument raged.

This isn't how it's supposed to be, one side complained.

He came back didn't he?

Yeah, but just like Tufan said, he can't wait to leave.

He said he's taking you along when he goes.

But what if he doesn't really want me?

He's your dad. He came back. He came back.

For me? Did he come for me?

For Gran. He came for Gran. That's what he said.

But she's staying. He's going back without her.

Maybe I don't want to go. Not without Gran.

"You seem to have a lot going on up here," Sophie said, tapping Aaron's forehead lightly. Her touch made him jump. He'd forgotten she was there.

"I...I was thinking."

"I can see that."

He looked up. Her black hair gleamed in the light of the fire. He couldn't help himself. He reached out, and when he touched it, it flowed between his fingers like dark water. She surprised him then by taking his hand and placing it on the large bump that was her belly. After a bit he jumped and pulled it away. Something under his palm had moved.

"Was that...? Was that the baby?"

She nodded. Then they smiled at each other the way people do when they share a secret.

"Why don't you tell me what's on your mind," she said softly.

"I've been worried...," he began, then stopped, not knowing how to go on.

"Start anywhere."

He took a breath. "How come sometimes my dad is so nice and shows me stuff, and sometimes he says, 'Get out of my way!' and 'Don't touch that!'?"

She sighed. "Your dad is a little like most people. He can be patient and kind, and funny and...and loving. But when he has things on his mind, and when he's busy, he can be as grumpy as a hibernating bear. Then it's best to stay out of his way."

"Like today?"

She smiled. "Just like today."

"Is he gonna be like that when I come to Dawson with you? 'Cause if he is, then I don't want to go. Then I want to stay here, with Gran."

For a long moment, Sophie stared at him. "Did your father ask you to come?"

"Yeah. When we had the man-to-man talk. He kept talking about 'when we go back to Dawson.' But I'm not sure. I'm not sure I want to go without Gran. Will he feel bad if I stay here?"

She hesitated. "I think that's something we should all discuss. It's a big decision, either way."

Aaron sat. A log shifted in the fireplace. Sparks exploded, flamed, then settled and faded. "Can I ask you something else?" he said.

"Sure. What else do you want to know?"

"How come my dad stayed away so long? How come he didn't come back before?"

"That," said Sophie, "is a fair question, but it's best answered by your father."

From upstairs came the sound of boxes being shifted and his father's voice. "For crying out loud!" he said. Then he added some words Aaron wasn't allowed to say.

Sophie squeezed his hand. "Probably today's not the best day to ask."

TWENTY-SIX

Aaron wanted to help pick up Gran from the hospital, but after seeing his dad so grumpy the night before, he was afraid to ask. He was afraid his dad would say, "No, you can't miss any more school." So he asked Sophie, and she smiled and said, "Of course you can come."

They called a taxi and his father sat in the front with the driver. He was unusually quiet. It was Sophie who answered Aaron's questions about Dawson.

"In the summer," she began, "the sun never sets. It's shining before you get up in the morning and it's still shining after you go to bed at night. It gets a little gray around two o'clock in the morning, but it never gets dark. The winter's not nearly as appealing.

It's dark most of the day and all night, and the nights are long. But that's when you see the northern lights. They dance across the heavens in ribbons of color. People come from all over the world to see them."

Aaron sat beside her, listening. Outside, the stores of Gerrard Street flashed by. "It's nothing like this," Sophie said with a sigh as they passed windows agleam with lights and rainbow displays of saris. "Most of our shopping is done from a catalogue."

"I don't do a lot of shopping," Aaron said.

"Tell me about your concert," Sophie said. So Aaron told her how he and Tufan were going to be making the introductions. "Mr. Collins said I could save you seats near the front, in case you want to take pictures or something."

That was when his dad spoke up. "We'll take a video," he said. "I brought my camera. That way Gran won't miss out even if she doesn't feel up to coming along."

* * *

When they arrived at her room, Gran was seated in a wheelchair, dressed and ready to go. She asked Aaron to push her down the hall, and he did, walking as carefully as he could so as not to bump into anything.

There was a wait for the elevator, and when it came, the people inside made room for them. Gran's chair ended up facing one that was being pushed by a young man in a hospital uniform.

"Oh my goodness. It is that helpful boy again," said a familiar voice, and Aaron saw that the woman in the other chair was Tufan's grandmother. "You were right," she said smiling. "The doctors here are taking good care of me."

"Are you going home now, like my gran?" Aaron said.

"Not yet. Today this young man is taking me for X-rays. Then we will see."

She smiled at Gran. "I am Amina," she said.

Gran smiled back and said, "Hello, Amina, I'm Fran."

"You are fortunate to be going home already. I think your grandson must have been missing you."

"Yes," Gran said as she turned her head to smile at Aaron. "And I missed him."

"I am missing my grandson too." She leaned toward Gran. "We are so fortunate," she said. "To have our grandsons close."

"We certainly are," Gran agreed.

The elevator door swished open then, and everybody said goodbye as they filed out.

"How do you know that lady?" Gran asked.

"She's Tufan's grandmother. Once, when I was in the office making announcements, she brought his lunch to school. And she came to the hospital in the ambulance the day I broke my arm."

"Tufan? Is he a friend of yours?"

"He's in my class," he said, not really answering the question. Then he smiled because he realized if he moved to Dawson, Tufan wouldn't be in his class ever again.

* * *

That afternoon Aaron went back to school. At the end of the day, Mr. Collins told the two boys to meet him by the gym doors for a quick stage rehearsal, and that's why they were leaning against the wall not far from each other.

They didn't speak until Tufan said, "The man who picked you up yesterday? That was your dad, huh?"

"Yeah, that was my dad." Aaron hoped Tufan wasn't going to say anything mean about his father.

"So what'd he bring you, besides the key chain?"

"What?"

"Well, he's been gone for years. Didn't he bring you anything?"

Aaron wasn't sure how to answer. He didn't want to try explaining Sophie.

"I got a surprise," he said.

"Yeah? An iPod or something?"

"A computer. I got a computer. With a webcam," he said, remembering the new purchase.

"Oh yeah? You didn't have one?"

"No. This is my first."

"About time then."

Aaron was relieved. Tufan was just...talking...like he'd talk to anybody. It gave him the courage to say, "I'm glad your grandmother's getting better."

He was prepared to hear Tufan snarl, *You don't talk about my grandmother*. But Tufan said, "Me too. I was kind of worried when she got sick." He glanced at Aaron. "She told me you're a nice boy."

"She did?"

"Yeah. But then she doesn't know what a loser you are." He laughed, and Aaron wondered if that was a joke. Should he laugh too? He wasn't sure. He was relieved when Mr. Collins arrived.

The teacher took them through their rehearsal in no time. Everything went so well that they were done just after four o'clock. "Break a leg!" Mr. Collins said as they gathered their belongings.

Break a leg? Aaron didn't get that, but he heard Tufan call, "Thanks," on his way out of the gym, so he said, "Thanks," before he left too.

The school was quiet. The hallway leading to the outer door was empty. Aaron didn't notice. All he wanted to do was get home to see Gran and Sophie and his dad.

When he pushed against the door's crash bar, he saw Tufan outside, waiting. A worm of worry began to stir in Aaron's belly. Then he felt silly. They had just spent days writing and learning their poem. In all that time Tufan had hardly been mean at all. Aaron stepped out. Behind him the door made a whooshing sound. When it clicked shut, Tufan came closer.

"I...I hafta go home," Aaron said.

"Yeah, I know. Your daddy's waiting with more presents for you."

"No. I..." Aaron stopped, remembering Jeremy's advice.

"Does it hurt?" Tufan asked, motioning to the arm.

Aaron shook his head.

Tufan moved closer, trapping Aaron against the wall. "I can make it hurt," he said. The worm in Aaron's belly froze and turned into an icicle of fear. A soft whimper escaped his lips.

"Suck," Tufan said when he heard. Then he smiled.

Not a happy smile, Aaron thought. The icicle dug deeper. He took a gasping breath. "You'd better not… or…or else," he said, his voice quivering with fear.

"Else what? You gonna stop me?"

"I'm gonna tell. I'll tell everybody. And you'll be… suspended."

Tufan's eyebrows rose. "Who's gonna believe you? I'll tell them you fell. They know what a klutz you are. So you broke your arm all over again."

Aaron gasped. "Maybe…," he started. "Maybe I am a klutz. But they'll believe me anyway." And then, because *he* believed, his voice grew stronger. "Everybody will believe me. Karen…Mrs. Matthews will believe me! Mr. Collins will believe me! Even Mr. Ulanni will believe me!"

Tufan shifted. Aaron glanced around. There was no one in the schoolyard, but he no longer cared that they were alone. He took a new breath and his voice got louder as he said, "And…and Jeremy, he'll believe me. And Sophie and my dad and my gran, they'll believe me too." Then he rose to his tiptoes and leaned into Tufan's face. "And your grandmother! She'll believe me. She thinks I'm nice. You said so. *She'll* believe me."

Tufan's mouth opened, but no sound came out.

"And you should close your mouth! You'd look smarter," Aaron finished.

Tufan's mouth closed. Then he laughed. "You're such a dweeb," he said. "Can't you take a joke?"

Then he turned and, to Aaron's relief, walked away.

TWENTY-SEVEN

All the way home, Aaron wondered about Tufan. Was that a joke? He wasn't sure, but he felt good because, joke or no joke, he had stood up for himself.

When he got to his house, he found the front door locked. Instead of ringing the doorbell, he used his key and let himself in. He was taking off his boots when he heard voices in the kitchen.

"Things are so much better this year," Gran was saying. "His teacher's wonderful, and he's getting counseling."

She's talking about me, Aaron thought. A flicker of worry stirred in his chest. He didn't like it when his gran talked to other people about him. And now she was probably talking to his dad and Sophie. What was she telling them?

"Paul, his Big Brother, has been a huge help," Gran went on. "And, for the first time ever, he has a friend. You don't know what a difference that makes."

That didn't sound bad. Maybe she was telling only good things.

"But it's been...up and down," Gran continued. "Lately there have been more ups, but it doesn't take much to set him off. You've seen that for yourselves. He still gets excited."

Aaron groaned. He didn't want to hear that.

"How's he doing at school?" his father asked.

"Oh, Aaron's smart enough, I've told you that before. He's smarter than most people realize. But his behavior is such a distraction that sometimes that's all they see."

"It can't have been easy for you," Sophie said.

"Easy? When he was four, getting him through the school doors was a daily battle."

Aaron knew what was coming. *Don't...don't tell*, he thought as he let his backpack slide to the floor.

But Gran went on. "There we were on his first morning, everybody lined up and excited, and Aaron refused to go inside. He sat down on the pavement, and I couldn't budge him. His teacher came and tried to coax him in, but that didn't work. The principal came. He wanted to pick Aaron up and carry him inside, and Aaron said, 'Keep your hands off me, perv.' I near died of embarrassment."

Aaron squirmed. That's how he was feeling. Like he wanted to die of embarrassment. He sloughed off his coat and let it fall on top of the backpack.

"It took almost a month before he walked through the school doors without making a fuss," Gran went on. "I was afraid they'd tell me to keep him home. But they didn't. Have to give them credit. They've done their best to cope with him."

Aaron walked toward the kitchen, hoping Gran would stop when she saw him. But as he came closer, he heard his father's voice. "I should have been here. I didn't...I couldn't...I...I'm sorry."

"Sorry!" Aaron sputtered as he pushed open the kitchen door. "You said...you said sorry's not enough! And it's not! It's not enough!" he shouted as he glared at his father. When he spoke again, his words were quieter, but every bit as sharp. "Where were you? Where were you, anyway?"

His father exhaled a great breath and sank into his chair like a balloon leaking air.

"Tell him," Sophie urged.

"Yeah! Tell me! Tell me where…where you were… and why…why you never—" His throat tightened. He choked back a sob.

His father's hands sagged into his lap while Aaron struggled for breath.

"Like Sophie said," his father finally began, "this family has too many secrets. *I* have too many secrets. What I haven't told you is that I stayed away because I was ashamed to come home. I was ashamed," he said again. "When I left, I just wanted to run. I couldn't get far enough away."

"From me? You ran from me?" Aaron said, his eyes bright with tears.

"Yes. From you," his dad admitted. "But all the time, I felt so bad about leaving." He looked at his hands. His fingers were twisting together like Aaron's worms.

"What I did was, I started to drink and then I didn't stop. I couldn't keep a job. I went from place to place trying to forget about Sarah, about…" He glanced at Aaron.

"You were trying to forget me?" Hot tears streaked down Aaron's cheeks. "I was remembering you! I remembered you every day! Why were you forgetting me?"

"I was trying to forget *myself*. The part of myself that couldn't cope. The part that couldn't help you."

Aaron gasped for air. He shook his head, trying to keep his thoughts clear. His dad was supposed to know stuff. His dad was supposed to tell him how to do things right. He took a big breath and wiped the tears off his face.

His father looked up. "When you're scared, *you* hide in a closet. I tried to hide in a bottle."

Aaron didn't get it. "You're too big to hide in a bottle," he said.

A bark of laughter exploded from his dad. "You've got that right," he said. "You've got that so right."

Turning to Gran, his dad said, "Mom, I know how disappointed you were, but I couldn't get anything right. I know I was a bad son, a lousy husband." He turned to Aaron. "And I was useless as a father."

"Oh, Liam," Gran said, and Aaron saw that her face was wet with tears too.

"Don't feel sorry for me," his father said. "I don't deserve that. What I did, I did to myself. You know that story I told you about meeting Sophie? What I didn't tell you is that it really *was* a story. There was no bear. I was so drunk, I ran into a sharp blade and had to be carried into the nursing station. If it wasn't for Herb and Sophie,

I would have bled to death that night. As it was, I don't actually remember being stitched up."

"No bear?" Aaron said.

"Not that day," his father said.

Aaron was disappointed. He looked at Sophie, hoping she'd say, *Of course there was a bear*, but she stayed silent and her eyes never left his father's face.

"When I came to," his dad said, "I realized I had hit rock bottom. It was Sophie who helped me get off the bottle. When I was finally dry, I got a job, a good job, and I asked her to marry me." He grinned at her then. "She said *no*. Told me I had to be dry for two years before she'd even think of it. So I dried out, and we got married last March."

"But that was good news. Why on earth didn't you tell us that?" Gran asked.

"I—," he started. "I was happy, for the first time in years. I didn't want to spoil that by telling Sophie about the mess I'd made. I was afraid if I told her of the life I'd left behind, she wouldn't have me. And I was afraid to tell you about her, because I knew you'd want to talk to her and meet her, and then she'd know...everything."

When he reached across the table to Sophie, she took his hands and he held them before he turned back to Aaron. "You think you're a loser? Look at me.

Nothing you've done comes close." He paused. "Anyway, now you know. I could give you the details, but they're not pretty, and I'd just as soon forget them myself. I did a lot of things wrong. Not being a good father to you was the worst."

For what seemed a long time, nobody spoke. Aaron stood staring at his dad. So many secrets. He wasn't sure now he'd wanted to hear them all.

It was his father who spoke first. "Aaron," he said. He paused, then started again. "Son, Sophie tells me there's something else I've messed up."

Just as if lightning had flashed across the sky, Aaron knew what his father was going to say next. He wobbled. He felt as if he had been dropped in the toilet and the water was swirling. He stopped breathing, waiting to be flushed away.

It was a relief to feel hands on his shoulders. Gran's hands. She made room for him on her chair and pulled him down to sit beside her. She sat like a wall, straight and tall, for him to lean on, when his father said, "It's about your coming with us to Dawson. To tell you the truth, I've been such a lousy father for so long, the idea of taking you along never occurred to me."

"I guess I'm a little too weird," Aaron said in a small voice. He laughed then as if it was a joke.

Something to hide behind when his father told him he didn't want him around.

"You obviously don't know much about Dawson," his dad said. "When you get there, you'll find out real quick that we've got all kinds of personalities up there. After all, I live there. I think you'll fit right in."

"What?" Now he wasn't sure what his dad was saying.

"Liam means that right now our house is too small, and we can't take you along when we leave," Sophie said. "We've only got two rooms. But with the baby coming, we already have plans to add on."

"When we're done, we'll have room for you and for Gran too," his father went on. "You can come. Both of you. To visit. To get to know us. So we can get to know you. And after that? We'll see what happens after that. I want to be a better dad, for you and for the new baby." He stopped.

Aaron leaned against Gran as he tried to sort through everything he'd heard. His dream of having a full-time dad here at home was gone. He sighed. Tufan would laugh. He'd say, "Didn't I tell you?"

Then Aaron remembered a word his dad had used. "Visit?" he said. "We can visit?"

Sophie smiled and nodded.

Aaron turned to look at Gran. "D'you want to go?" he asked.

"I'd love to," she said. "After all, there'll be a new grandchild to hold."

"Gran and I will be delighted to come," Aaron said, using words he'd heard or read somewhere. He wasn't sure why they made everybody laugh.

That's when Sophie came over and wrapped her arms around Aaron. "Your gran has been right all along," she said. "You're much smarter than people give you credit for."

Aaron grinned and tried hard not to twitch away.

TWENTY-EIGHT

On Thursday morning Mr. Collins handed the boys their costumes. Tufan grimaced when he saw them. There were two short green tunics trimmed with gold braid and one red jester's hat with tiny bells on each of the points.

"I'm not wearing a fool's hat!" Tufan said.

Mr. Collins smiled. "It's not for you," he said. "I got that for Aaron."

"I'm gonna be the fool?" Aaron asked.

"We're all fools sometimes," Mr. Collins said.

"Typecasting," Tufan mumbled.

Aaron wasn't sure what that meant. "Yeah. Typecasting," he echoed.

Tufan made a kind of snorting noise.

The boys tried on their tunics, and Mr. Collins helped Aaron put on the hat. "Think about this," he said as he tied it under Aaron's chin. "Fools have been making people laugh since the beginning of time, and there's nothing like laughter to make our troubles feel smaller."

Aaron nodded. The little bells on his hat chimed.

"Do you hear that?" Mr. Collins said. "The bells are there for a reason. They're going to remind you to stand still. If you hear them, you'll know that you're moving too much and you have to stop."

"And if you don't...," Tufan began, his voice sounding mad.

Mr. Collins cleared his throat, and for some reason the sound stopped whatever Tufan was going to say. "Yeah," he said more kindly. "So don't be a ding-a-ling. Stand still."

"Ding-a-ling," Aaron said with a chuckle. "I won't be a ding-a-ling." And he stood so still that the bells stopped ringing.

* * *

That evening Aaron was in the change room struggling to place the hat on his head when Tufan walked in.

"Give it here," he said, snatching the hat from Aaron's hands.

"Hey! It's mine!" Aaron said, trying to grab it back.

Tufan held it out of reach. "I don't want the hat, turkey. I'm just trying to help, 'cause, you know, you can't tie it with one hand."

Feeling a little foolish, Aaron stopped moving and let Tufan place the hat on his head. "Thanks," he said when the strings were tied under his chin. The little bells ting-tanged.

"You're welcome," Tufan grunted. "I figure if fools make people happy, you're gonna rock. Just don't mess this up and make a fool of me too."

* * *

When they stepped out of the change room, Ms. Masilo had the whole choir standing in line. She was pacing back and forth on her black high heels, smiling, but sounding angry every time she had to remind someone to stop talking.

When they saw the boys, the kids began to laugh. "What are you supposed to be?" Jeremy asked.

"Messengers," Tufan said.

"What's your message?" Karima wanted to know.

"It's in here," Aaron said, tapping his finger against the side of his head so that all his bells rang.

"Uh-oh," Horace said. "A message from inside Aaron's head. There's a scary thought." His words made even Aaron laugh.

"Quiet! Quiet! Quiet!" Ms. Masilo warned. Then she directed them into the gym and onto the stage.

The audience settled back as the choir filed in, but when Tufan and Aaron stepped to the front of the stage, there were whispers and chuckles. The boys waited. When the room was silent, Aaron said, "Welcome. Welcome to our *Voices of Winter* concert."

Then Tufan set the beat, and Ms. Masilo's hands came up. When they dropped, the choir chanted:

Turn it off! Turn it off! Turn that noisy phone right off!
Turn it off! Turn it off! Turn that noisy phone right off!

There was laughter from the audience. Then Aaron began:

'Twas the night of the concert, the kids were all thrilled
To stand on the stage as the chairs quickly filled
With families who talked and moved all around,
But once the show started, there wasn't a sound.

Then, just as the choir began singing their song,
A cell phone rang out with a tune loud and long.
It bothered the audience, it pealed through the room,
Distracted the kids, made Ms. Masilo fume.

He paused, letting the choir repeat their opening lines.

Turn it off! Turn it off! Turn that noisy phone right off!
Turn it off! Turn it off! Turn that noisy phone tight off!

Aaron used the break to peer past the stage lights. He was looking for his dad and Sophie. Then he saw them. They were in the third row. He wanted to call out and wave, but when he lifted his hand, the bells on his hat began ringing. A small wave of panic washed over him. He glanced at Mr. Collins standing on the floor in front of the stage, right where he said he would be. His teacher smiled and nodded. Aaron took a breath. Beside him, Tufan was beating the drum, strong and steady. He refocused, and when Ms. Masilo gave him the sign, he began the next verse.

She tapped her baton, stopped the choir's cheery singing,
And still, from the room that cell phone kept ringing.

Then he stopped, and just like in practice, from Mr. Collins's pocket came the sound of a phone ringing. There was more laughter in the audience. When it stopped, Aaron continued.

Then she turned, and she frowned, and she coughed a loud cough.
"Your phone is a pain, sir," she growled. "Turn it off!"

So ladies and gentlemen, listeners all,
Turn your little phones off and don't take that call.
Chat on your own time. And just for today,
Please hear us sing, see us dance, watch our play.

When the choir repeated the last two lines, everybody joined in to chant:

Turn it off! Turn it off! Turn that noisy phone right off!
Turn it off! Turn it off! Turn that noisy phone right off!

The audience laughed and clapped. The boys bowed. Mr. Collins gave them a thumbs-up sign, and Ms. Masilo smiled and smiled. Aaron looked at her. Was she smiling happy this time? He couldn't tell. But everybody else was, he was sure of that.

There was a great rustling and shuffling in the audience as people checked to make sure their cell phones were off. Aaron and Tufan took their places, one on each side of the stage. When everyone was quiet again, the class began to sing.

Aaron felt great. Like something big inside him was abuzz with happiness. The buzzy part of him wanted to jump up and down for joy, but he didn't. He stood still. So still that the bells on his hat hardly rang at all. Only his eyes moved to the third row, and with the smile still wide on his face, he saw Sophie smile back. His father didn't. He was too busy filming so Gran could see everything too.

TWENTY-NINE

At the end of February the schoolyard was still dotted with patches of ice. Some days the sun seemed brighter, but that didn't stop the north wind from whistling around the building. Aaron stood at the library window, searching for signs that the seasons were changing.

"Look," he said to Jeremy, pointing to a robin perched on the branch of a maple tree.

"The poor thing looks frozen," Jeremy said.

"Yeah, but it's a sign of spring, and after spring comes summer. This summer we're going to Dawson."

Jeremy grinned. "As if I didn't know. You've only told me maybe a thousand times."

"Yeah," Aaron said. "I can't wait."

When Mrs. Evans called everybody to the carpet, the boys hurried to sit down, Aaron in his spot, Jeremy beside him. "Is it a story? Is it a new story?" Aaron asked.

"It's a poem," Mrs. Evans said. "One I think you, in particular, will enjoy."

"I bet you can't wait to hear it," Tufan said. "Cantwait can't wait!" he said.

Aaron turned. "That joke is so old it's dead," he said. To his surprise, Tufan looked embarrassed.

When Mrs. Evans told them the poem was written by a Canadian named Robert Service, Aaron's hand shot up. "My dad told me about him. He used to live in Dawson. That's where my dad lives too. In Dawson. And Sophie and baby Fran. And this summer we're going to visit them. Me and my gran."

"People will head for the hills when they hear you're coming," Tufan said.

"Nope. Not gonna happen," Aaron said. "Those people up there are really nice. I talked to them already. On the webcam. My dad introduced me to lots of them."

Mrs. Evans placed her hand on Aaron's shoulder. "I'll make you a deal, Aaron," she said. "Why don't *I* read the poem and *you* listen. And when I'm done, *you* can tell us a little more about Dawson and *we'll* listen."

"Okay," Aaron said, and Mrs. Evans began:

There are strange things done in the midnight sun
By the men who moil for gold;
The Arctic trails have their secret tales
That would make your blood run cold;
The Northern Lights have seen queer sights,
But the queerest they ever did see
Was the night on the marge of Lake Lebarge
I cremated Sam McGee.

In no time, Aaron found himself lost in the words that told of the north. The world where stars danced heel and toe across the night sky. The world his father, and Sophie, and baby Fran called home. *I can't wait. I can't wait,* he thought. Then he stopped, realizing what he was thinking. He straightened. Lifted his head. *Yes, I can,* he told himself. *I can. I can. Aaron Can Wait.*

ACKNOWLEDGMENTS

Nothing I've ever accomplished has happened without help.

So, to Richard Unger, who said, "Write a sequel," thereby planting the seed.

To Peter Carver and the writers in his class, who shared their wisdom.

To the gifted women in my writing group: Carolyn Beck, Anne Laurel Carter, Kristyn Dunnion and Cheryl Rainfield, who read, reread and shared invaluable insights.

To the staff and students at Agnes Macphail Public School, who have helped launch my books and made thoughtful suggestions. (With special thanks to Andrew Li, who pointed out the need for laughter, and Dita Irawan, who suggested I might want to "consider Aaron's perspective.")

To June Brown, Goldie Spencer and Connie Hubbarde, who listened.

To Cathy Comisky, who shared the discoveries on the Gold Rush Trail.

To Peter Kerz, who brought home the frogs and toads that led to the great worm escape.

To Susanne Farrow, who shares her love of music with students of all abilities and only smiles happy smiles.

To my editor, Sarah Harvey, who guides with a gentle hand, and to all the people at Orca Book Publishers who have labored to produce this book.

THANK YOU!

ANNA KERZ's first book, *The Mealworm Diaries*, was shortlisted for many awards, including a Ruth and Sylvia Schwartz Award. Anna is also the author of *The Gnome's Eye*, a story loosely based on her experiences as an immigrant child. When she's not writing, Anna is collecting and telling stories to audiences of all ages. She lives in Scarborough, Ontario, with her husband, Frank, and their dog, Bailey.